PRAISE FOR
VIRGINIA'S WAR

A fascinating glimpse into WWII on the home front…There are schemers, boot-leggers, corrupt politicos, and black marketeers aplenty. a wonderful read about an amazing chapter in history that has affected us all and continues to influence the world of today.　　　　— **Nancy Pendleton, Examiner**

A rich and complex conflict between a mix of people using social expectations and scandals, and he brings it to a boil by compressing it into a tiny town. How-ever, the town loses its innocence and insulation from the harshness of the war as battle impacts the lives of its sons.

　　　　— **John Monteith, author of the *Rogue Submarine series***

"London's nearly poetic prose weaves several apparently separate stories into a convergence and a surprise ending." — **Walter Shiel, author of *Once a Knight: A Novel of Aerial Combat & Romance in World War I***

"ENORMOUS IN EVERY WAY! Jack Woodville London delivers a historical Masterpiece of war, politics, love, and betrayal."

　　　　— **Geri Ahearn, author and blogger**

An engaging and edgy look at life in a small down during World War II, London captures the delicate and sometimes sinister intricacies of little town USA.

　　　　— **The Book Connection**

Awards:
London Book Festival, Silver Medal for General Fiction
Author of the Year, Military Writers Society of America
Stars and Flags Book Award, Silver Medal

FRENCH LETTERS©

BOOK ONE

VIRGINIA'S WAR
Tierra, Texas 1944

A Novel, By

JACK WOODVILLE LONDON

Published by Vire Press, Austin, Texas
www.virepress.com
Editor-in-chief: Mindy Reed, The Authors' Assistant

Library of Congress Cataloging-in Publication Data

London, Jack W. 1947-
French Letters, Virginia's War: Tierra, Texas 1944/ Jack Woodville London

p.   cm.
ISBN 978-0-9906121-3-1

1.   World War II—Home front
2.   Texas—Family life—World War II
3.   Domestic Families—Fiction

Fic Lon   PS642 L86 2008   20080821

10 9 8 7 6 5 4 3
Original Copyright @ 2008 Jack Woodville London

Printed in the United States of America

To my mother,
Martha Emalea Myers London.

Mother was among those thousands of women who fought World War II on the home front with selfless sacrifice and dedication to her family and country. Later, as a widow, Mother returned to earn a university degree, to teach school, and to become a playwright. Mother decidedly was not Virginia Sullivan but she did have her own war story. She, and it, inspired me to write Virginia's War as the first book of French Letters.

ACKNOWLEDGMENT

To my dear wife Alice, without whose support I would not have been able to write at all, and to my fellow Saint-Céréans, whose encouragement, patience, collaboration, and contributions kept me at work, I acknowledge my gratitude for making Virginia's War possible. Its flaws are entirely mine but its completion is thanks to you.

PROLOGUE

It hadn't been bad, not as funerals go, although not without a bit of drama. Even so, the Grummans were quiet afterward, during the procession to the cemetery, back at the reception the church ladies had put on in the fellowship hall, in the car on the way home. Not all the Grummans had gone to the funeral, just George and Lucille; the older boys lived too far away and Togg, well, he just didn't go. It was Lucille who spoke first.

"Are you okay?"

"I'm okay."

She didn't think he was okay. George was as old as Doc had been, a year or two one way or the other, and they had been friends ever since Doc had moved to Bridle a couple of years after the war. They used to call him "New Doc," but that had been a long time ago. No one remembered that, just Lucille and George.

"It was nice, the way Frank spoke," she ventured.

Frank had spoken about Doc the way any son would, but better. His eulogy had led each person in the church to a personal memory of Doc, stories of his having given the boys their football physical exams and of having delivered the girls' babies, of school board meetings and raffles, the stuff of their small town lives. Even after he retired Doc had asked nearly everyone in town at one time or another when they were going to come up to Colorado and go fishing with him. Everyone had a Doc story.

"And then bringing out those things — I never saw anything like it!"

Frank had been a little theatrical. As he was speaking he brought out some of Doc's mementos and displayed them from the pulpit: Doc's old fishing gear, a silk map, a set of bound books — things that Doc had given Frank barely a week before. Lucille thought that it had been a loving touch but she already had forgotten precisely what the items were because of what Frank had done next.

"And then he plucked that photograph out of those books. How did he say it? Ah, 'the only old picture I have of my parents, how they looked before Dad went off to the war.'" Lucille shook her head slowly. "Poor Virginia."

George was still quiet; that was mostly George's way. Lucille sensed that he had become tense, his mouth pursed and eyes narrowed; that was mostly Lucille's way.

"When he showed everybody that picture, all blown-up poster size, Doc in his uniform and Virginia there in that dress, her hair done up in a shingle — did you know we used to call that a shingle? On the porch there. Do you think that was her house back in, wherever it was they used to live before the war?"

"Tierra."

"Tierra. Poor Virginia, that was so awful."

Lucille said that it was awful; in truth it was exactly what people in a small town wanted in a funeral, the widow bolting up from the pew, hysterical screams and guttural sobs. She believed that Virginia would have thrown herself across Doc's open casket if Peter, the other son, sitting with her, hadn't held her back. Lucille had known Virginia for almost sixty years; everyone knew everyone in Bridle, but Virginia never had been able to shake off the cloak the town had put on her as an outsider.

"That picture of the two of them, really…" Lucille didn't know quite what revealing the picture had done to Virginia but it had been enough to snap something inside.

Everyone had admired the picture. Someone had put it up on an easel so that it, too, could be viewed when the friends passed into the community hall to tell Virginia and the boys how sorry they were for their loss.

"I told her how handsome Doc was in his uniform," Lucille rattled on. "She was pretty enough when she was a girl, but Doc... Well, I can see why she fell for him."

"Did you hear them?"

"Hear who?"

"The boys. Frank. And Peter."

Lucille had heard them. The men had carried Doc's casket out of the church to the black coach that would lead them to the cemetery. While the family was getting into the limousine for the procession, Peter had grabbed Frank by the shoulder, spun him around, and hissed at him:

"You bastard! You just had to hurt Mother with your goddamned pictures and stories, didn't you! You want a story? How about the one about the French whore? It's a true one — you are the son of a bitch, a fucking war orphan! I mean it. And I'm through putting up with you. Trust me, I'll get you."

Peter's face had been bent with anger, eyes flashing, jaw clenched. Then, in less than five seconds, it was over. Peter had slipped into the limousine beside his wife, patting her hand, straightening his uniform, his face already masked with an expression both solicitous and grieving. He had not meant for the Grummans to hear.

The Grummans parked in their driveway, shut off the engine, and went inside. George had built the house right after the war, three rooms. They had added here and there over the years but the kitchen was still tiny, just enough space for the old gas range and an "ice box," as they called it. When Lucille put their coffee cups on the table the clink of spoon on china rang through the empty house.

"I heard it," Lucille finally answered. "It was ugly, Peter losing his temper like that. He always had a temper. And to call Frank that… I never, and in front of everybody. Do you think anyone else heard? Lord, I hope not."

George sipped the coffee, loosened his collar button, and let out a long, slow sigh. He had quit smoking a long time ago but never had got his breath back. Lucille thought the sigh was just one of his breathing spells.

"Virginia, wailing like that, that's what set him off." George sat, arms crossed, coffee getting cold in the cup. "Peter never did have any sense. Did anyone else hear him? I don't know. I think everyone else was already walking to their cars."

"People used to say such ugly things," Lucille whispered.

"They did," George nodded. "But that was right after they moved here. And that was a long time ago."

"I think everybody's forgotten the rumors. And Peter was, well, he was just being hateful. He was always like that."

"He was," George agreed. "He was. I don't think anything will come of it."

He hoped not; it *had* been a long time ago. People, he figured, had gotten over their talking about other people and people also had gotten over being talked about. The rumors had wounded but the wounds had healed. Doc was dead. Virginia, well, she wasn't dead, but she was in a retirement home somewhere, wherever it was that Peter lived. Frank was down in Austin. It couldn't matter any more.

"And," Lucille finished, "nobody knows, not really." She sipped her coffee, too, and then saw how tired her husband looked. "Don't worry, dear. They don't know."

"They don't," he said. *Not even you, Lucille, dear,* he said to himself. *You don't know the half of it.*

They sat in the kitchen of their empty house, drinking coffee and waiting for the afternoon sun to go down, for the arrival of evening to cool them. They expected, but didn't really believe, that someone might drop in on them, but no one did, not then nor in the next few days. Eventually Lucille heard at the beauty shop that the family, or families, had gone home, Frank and his wife back to Austin, Peter and his wife, their children, and Virginia, all back to Colorado. None of the town gossips had mentioned Peter's outburst, or anything else.

By and by, things seemed to return to normal and one day, weeks later, the Grummans dared to think that nothing more would come of it.

FRENCH LETTERS©

※

BOOK ONE

VIRGINIA'S WAR
Tierra, Texas 1944

CHAPTER ONE

⚜

March 1944

They saw the enemy patrol race across the road and disappear behind the shell of the burned out barn. There was no choice but to give chase, even though they would be exposed as they ran. Sandy turned to the squad, stooped down slightly, then waved his hand over his shoulder and pointed to the barn. "Follow me," he yelled. Sandy sprinted across the road and dived to the ground under the ledge of a boarded-up window, then turned to make sure the squad made it across. It did. They caught their breath.

They listened but no sounds came from inside. Sandy duck-walked over to the door, listened, then pushed it with his foot. Nothing happened. He peeked through the doorway. The barn was empty.

"Okay, we'll edge around the corner. If there's any fire, cover me and I'll make a dash for it."

Sluggo nodded.

Sandy peered around the corner of the barn but drew no fire. He poked his rifle around the corner; again there was no response. Slowly, one foot at a time, he tiptoed around the building, then took off at a run across the field. The next cover was about thirty yards into the field, an old crumbling stone building he had noticed on reconnaissance. He took off for it, yelling "Cover me!" to Sluggo. He made it to the safety of the shelter, an abandoned cistern, then dived again to make himself as small a target as possible in case he had been sighted. After a few moments of silence, he turned and motioned for Sluggo to follow, then watched in agony as the private stumbled along at a leisurely pace, something like a mosey but with less urgency.

"You dick. You're gonna get us killed. Jesus."

"Don't blame me. This wasn't my idea. I didn't want to be here in the first place."

"You think those krauts are gonna just walk back to Berlin and tell Hitler they don't want to fight anymore? Hell no. Get up."

Sandy counted to three, then yelled, "Follow me!" again and took off at a dead run around the cistern and angled to the left toward the railroad tracks. He hadn't run ten steps before a grenade sailed past his head and exploded on the ground behind him and a hail of bullets whistled past. He jumped over a tangle of posts and barbed wire, ran another ten yards, and flung himself into a hollow, as good a foxhole as any. He landed on his stomach, his helmet pushed backward on his head, his rifle stock hitting him in the ribs. The impact knocked his breath out and he lay there for a minute, waiting as the flurry of fire died down. He couldn't spot the krauts.

When Sandy lifted his head up to peer over the edge of the foxhole a barrage of fire splattered all around him and nearly knocked his helmet off, prompting him to duck back in and burrow his stomach right into the dirt. *Where's Sluggo?* He had been right behind after they slipped out of the village and crossed the road, then charged into the field. Sluggo wasn't very tough; if he had been hit he would have screamed bloody murder. Sandy hazarded a quick glance up and backwards and, sure enough, Sluggo was holed up behind the pile of fence posts about ten yards back.

Sandy had no idea where the enemy was hidden and it scared him. *I smell 'em.* He had searched the barn, taking care to not raise his head above window level, nudging in the door with his boot rather than kick it open. He remembered what Sarge had told them, that when they searched a building, even if there weren't any krauts hiding inside, kicking the door would make so much racket that the Nazis hiding outside would know where you were. Sarge had told 'em right: the next time they went out on patrol Mike had kicked in the door of a tool shed. They found him in the alley. He had taken it right between the eyes.

He tried to remember the lay of the land, another thing Sarge had said over and over. "Pick your spots, then see what's left. Even if there ain't no krauts there when you move in, they might come up and dig in when you ain't lookin'." He remembered the stand of trees. *How far was it? Twenty yards? Maybe fifteen?* And the old stone cistern over to the right. He decided they wouldn't have circled back there and besides, if they had been using the cistern for defense then, in order to fire, they would have had to step out from the side where they would be exposed. *Sluggo, even Sluggo, would have made mince meat of them.* They had to be somewhere else when they fired. What was left?

Wherever they were, one thing was sure — they had him sighted in. Mortar rounds rained down around him; none hit. Even so, from their direction he could tell that the mortar was close and off to the left. *What was off to the left?* He thought hard, tried to remember. A fence? Another outbuilding? A barn? No, the barn, what was left of it, was beyond the cistern, and on the right. It was too far away. *The railroad tracks? Maybe.* He looked back to the fence posts.

"PSSST!"

He waited for Sluggo, then hissed again.

"PSSST! Hey, you still alive back there?"

"Whatcha want?" came a weary reply.

"You see where they are?"

"They're behind the big old weeds growin' over there. I seen 'em dive in behind."

"Over where?"

"Behind the cattle chute."

"The what?"

"You know, where they drive the cattle up to load on the trains."

He remembered. There was a cattle chute standing all by itself in the field, right next to the tracks. It was covered up by weeds and he had forgotten about it. But it was close enough to conceal the mortar and still be in range.

"You got any ammo left?"

"A little."

"They ain't seen you."

"So what."

"They don't know where you are. I'm gonna fool 'em."

Sandy felt around the edges of the foxhole, found a big clod, and picked it up with his free hand. The clod was pretty dry; it would likely fall apart when it hit. He slowly rolled over on his back so that he could loft it up and away without having to get up on his knees. If they were at the cattle chute and Sluggo was behind the pile of fence posts, he should throw the clod to his left which, now that he was on his back, would be his right. If he had it figured right the Germans would see the clod or hear it hit, then rain the mortar down on it. Sluggo would be in the clear to fire.

"PSST."

"What?"

"I'm gonna trick 'em. I'm gonna make 'em think you're off to the left. They'll think you're over there and start firing. When they do, stand up and hit 'em with everything you got. When you do, I'll charge at 'em and you follow me."

"You're stupid, you know that? You're gonna get us killed," Sluggo hissed.

"You got any better ideas?" He hated it when Sluggo went out on patrol with him. They had been killed three times already, and the war had just started. Sandy counted to three and hurled the clod up and off to his right.

"NOW," he shrieked. "NOW!"

He heard Sluggo yell "Take this! And this and this and this," and Sandy jumped to his feet, heading for the cattle chute as fast as he could run.

The krauts yelled back. "YAH! YAH! You're dead. Take this!" and sure enough, they had his range. Sandy ran to his right, darted left, then right again, and made it to the corner posts of the cattle chute. Sluggo ran up behind.

"YOU'RE DEAD! SURRENDER OR YOU'RE DEAD!"

The krauts didn't surrender. They had a cache of missiles and grenades and unleashed them faster than Sandy had ever seen before. He yelled at Sluggo for back up. Sluggo backed up. When he didn't hear any fire from behind him, Sandy turned and there was Sluggo, running away from the battle as fast as he could run.

"YOU TURD! GET BACK HERE!"

Sluggo speeded up.

"SLUGGO! DAMN YOU! I'VE GOT 'EM SURROUNDED, AND..."

A roar filled the air, a thunder so loud that it shook their heads inside their helmets and billowed their shirts in the wind. The krauts stopped, stood up, and shielded their eyes against the glaring sun. Sandy and Sluggo dropped to the ground and covered their heads as the roar increased to the sound of a hundred freight trains unleashed on the battlefield. From behind them a formation of warplanes swooped across the town, then the road. It dived in formation straight at the railroad tracks, then pulled up and climbed at full power. The sound was deafening. As they looked up they saw the doors of the bomb bay opening wide. Machine guns poked out from turrets.

Sandy grinned — the battle was over. The planes, coming from the west, were his. Nothing could defeat a wing of B-24's, the fastest, the most powerful, the loudest airplane in the world. He stood, shook the dirt off his clothes, and watched the planes bank to the left, then level off and race away to the north.

"IT'S OVER," he said, turning to make prisoners out of the krauts. "Come out with your hands...."

Splat.

A clod, a really hard clod, hit him in the nose and splattered dirt and some cow flop all over his face. The dirt streaked down and was washed into rivulets by the blood that gushed from his nose. He dropped back to the ground and covered his face, wiping the blood on his tee shirt.

Butch and the others ran up from the cattle ramp.

"Sorry, Sandy. Didn't mean to hurt you."

"You turd! You broke my nose. Jesus!" Sandy's nose was indeed a mess. Blood pumped away, sliming his cheeks with the less agreeable mixture that Butch had chosen as a last ditch bomb to turn the tide of battle. "Damn! We won — why'd you throw a rock after we won? Jesus!"

"Wasn't a rock. I said sorry."

Sandy pulled his football helmet off to get better access to his tee shirt which he used to wipe the mess off his face.

"It'll stop. Just lay down. Happens to me all the time."

The nose bleed didn't stop. The only consequence of Sandy laying down was that he landed on a prickly pear and got a back full of spines, making him jump back up, aggravating his bleeding and his sense of outrage.

"Why didn't you stop when the planes came over? We won. It's the rules." Sandy wadded his tee shirt into a ball and held it against his nose.

"Is not."

"Is too. They were B-24's. So they came from Clovis. So they were mine. If they were yours they would have been those clunky pieces of shit that come from Lubbock. I don't even know what they are. They've just got one engine."

Tommy spoke up for his side.

"Is not. One — you get one chance after an attack to throw one bomb. Two, even after a bomb run. Three, we did. It's the rules. And four. Well, there isn't a four. We won."

Butch chimed in:" You're the worst army in the world."

"Am not."

"Are too."

"Am not. Why don't we stick Sluggo on your army and see who wins?"

"Hey. We drew fair and square."

"Like fun. Three of you, two of me, and I get Sluggo. That ain't fair."

"It is fair. First, you drew American. Second, two of you and three Nazis should be a fair fight. Three, did you see the little turd run?"

"Saw you run when my bombers attacked. Hey! Those were my bombers. You're dead. And stop counting as if you were making up the rules."

The four soldiers argued rules of war while they wandered back across the railroad tracks toward Tierra. The main road into town from the Clovis

Highway led a couple of short blocks to the town square and the court-house. The nose bleed did not subside.

"Hey, Sandy, it looks like it's just gonna keep on gushin'. You need to go home."

"It'll stop. I'm just gonna sit down." He wandered over to the wooden sidewalk in front of Reilly's Grocery, then collapsed in a heap, his soaked tee shirt wrapped around his face. Dust blew across the square and settled on him and the others who stood next to him.

"Naw, really, it's still comin'. Why don't ya lay down? Ain't no cactuses here on the sidewalk."

Sandy did lie down, his bare back on the wide planks, feet dangling off the sidewalk and down on to the steps. Old Bradley's dog wandered across the street and wedged his way into the crowd of boys, then tried to lick Sandy's face.

"Get off me, you mutt. Damn. Now I've got dog slobber to go with mud and blood and cow shit." He shoved at the dog with his foot, which only made the dog more affectionate.

"When I get drafted I'm gonna fly planes," Sluggo ventured. He picked up Sandy's football helmet, tried it on, took it off, began to hand it to Sandy, then laid it back on the sidewalk.

"Don't be stupid. They don't let draftees fly planes. Draftees are grunts."

"What's a grunt?"

"Soldier. Grunts are soldiers. They're the soldiers who do the fightin!"

"What do you know about it?"

"Old Bradley told me." Old Bradley was the town's barber.

"What's he know about it?"

"I don't know. But he does. Anyway, only way you fly a plane is if you go to officer school. To go to officer school, you gotta go to college."

None of them were interested in college; their vague idea was that it was a worse form of school than the one they were already in.

A woman shrieked. They looked up.

"Oh my Goodness! Boys!"

It was Mrs. Tarlton, known to them as Old Lady Tarlton.

"Lie down, there, boy. And get that dog away; he's licking you. What's your name?" Mrs. Tarlton held a bag of groceries, which she handed to Butch who, not knowing what else to do, took it. "That's right, sweetie, don't drop it."

Sandy told her his name. None of the others said anything.

"Well, Sandy Clayton, my oh my. What on earth happened to you?"

No one said anything to that either. They believed in a general way that Old Lady Tarlton might not object to boys playing soldier, but they had no doubt that she would tell their mothers if she knew they were throwing rocks and clods at each other.

"How did you get so much mud on your face?" She made it her business. "And why are you out here on the sidewalk? We need to get you home and get your face cleaned up." By way of therapy she reached down and tried to lift Sandy's arm, causing his bloody tee shirt to fall away. Her stare was met by a plainly broken nose and a face covered with grimy blood.

"My goodness, have you been bleeding long? You boys shouldn't play like this. When did this happen?"

They hemmed and hawed, scuffing their feet before Sandy answered.

"Just a few minutes ago. I'll be all …" Sandy tried to talk his way out of it, but when he got to his feet he felt light-headed and began to sway. Before he could steady himself he sagged back down onto the sidewalk.

Mrs. Tarlton wheeled around to the others. "Run get his mother. Tell her I'm taking him to the doctor." She stamped her feet and Sluggo took off at a run. "And you!" She turned to Butch. "Take these groceries to my house and put them on the kitchen table. I'll be right along after I take Sandy Clayton to Doc's." It never occurred to her to wonder whether Butch knew where she lived or if he thought the door might be locked. He would know, and it would not be locked. "Come with me, you poor thing," she said in a finale to Sandy. With more grace than she had used to lift him the first time, she steadied him on his feet, then turned him to face where she wanted him to go and began to march him the two blocks to Doc Pritchard's office.

Doc's office was located behind a grimy little door in the old general building a block from the town square. At one time it had joined the drug store and pharmacy that opened directly onto the square. However, Doc's feud with Mr. Bivens had led to the permanent nailing of the passageway. Mrs. Tarlton nudged Sandy through Doc's front door and into his small waiting room.

"Doc! Yoo hoo? Hello?"

Sandy slumped onto the wooden chair next to the door. He hated coming to Doc Pritchard's more than going for a haircut, or even to church. At least Old Bradley, the barber, told dirty jokes when the grownups weren't around. Nothing good ever happened at Doc Pritchard's.

"Doc? Please come out," she pleaded. "You have a very hurt boy out here."

"How hurt?" A voice came through the wooden doorway that sealed off the waiting room. "I'm with someone. Come back later."

"I can't. He's bleeding. At least come out and stop the bleeding.'"

Between Mrs. Tarlton's smothering and Doc's growl, Sandy wanted to take his chances and just go home.

"I'll be all right. I think it's …"

"Shh, boy! Don't get yourself excited or it'll just bleed more. Hold your head back. Doc? Come out here and stop the bleeding and then you can take your own sweet time." She rapped on the clinic door to make it clear that she wasn't going away and, moments later, it opened. Doc Pritchard stormed into the room.

"Who's out here yelling? I told you I was with someone." He glanced round, taking in that there was only one old woman and one very bloody boy in the room. "Who are you? What the hell did you do to yourself? Lorena? This ain't your kid, is he? You ain't got any kids. Who the hell's kid is this?" He growled at both of them, then settled on Sandy. "Who are you? You deaf? What the hell is this stuff?"

"Sandy Clayton."

"Bob Clayton's kid?"

"Yes sir."

"Come here, dammnit." Doc seized Sandy with a good deal more force than Mrs. Tarlton had used and propelled him through the door into the clinic. Mrs. Tarlton tried to follow him but he turned and blocked her way. "Go tell his mother I've got him." He slammed the door in her face.

The clinic had only three rooms, the waiting room at front and two others. Sandy watched as Doc kicked a door open, then pushed him through it.

"Lay down there, boy." He pointed to an examining table covered with a stained sheet. "Hurry up, Goddamnit, you think you're the only patient I got? What's this on your face?"

"Mud. Blood."

"And cow shit. You think I don't know cow shit? What the hell were you doing? Shit wrestling? Stupid little prick," he muttered. Doc's bedside manner was not his best quality. Even so, he began to clean the boy's face with a cotton towel and rubbing alcohol. After he got most of the muck off he could see that blood continued to gush from both nostrils. He tilted Sandy's face and peered into his nostrils, then stuck his finger up Sandy's nose. This he swabbed with more alcohol, rubbed in some Vaseline, and packed cotton into the opening. "Lay down there and be quiet. It'll stop now if you'll quit fartin' around. Hold your nose with your fingers, both sides. If you don't stop bleeding I'll have to cut you open and sew it shut." He stormed out of the room.

Sandy lay there, afraid to move and afraid of what Doc would do when he came back. For the first few minutes he just held his nose. He swallowed occasionally and wished he hadn't, the rancid mixture of blood and alcohol sour in his throat, but he was afraid to spit it up or to stand up and clear his throat. Before long, the taste of blood dissipated and he thought the bleeding had stopped. He waited several more minutes, then grew bored and began to look around the room. Doc's medical equipment consisted of a white enamel cabinet, a sink, and an examining table. There was a scale with a ruler on it, which Sandy remembered from earlier humiliations when Doc would glare at him, then call him a runt. On a wall next to the chair there was a rubber hose with a blood pressure cuff and a thing that looked like a thermometer. The cabinet supported several bottles of alcohol and Merthiolate and jars of cotton and swabs. Sandy noticed that the walls were pale green — slime green, he would tell Butch and Sluggo. The frosted glass window to the street was cracked and covered with masking tape. Sandy closed his eyes and wondered what he would tell his mother.

He must have dozed off, he thought, because a commotion in the next room startled him and he sat upright on the table, then tasted blood dribbling back down his throat. He heard a rattling of chairs on the floor, an indistinct rustle of people moving about, the hum of voices speaking too low to be understood. He swallowed hard and, finding no more blood, raised his head. Doc had left his door open; Sandy peeked to see if the old quack was coming. He didn't want to admit it but he did wish that his mother was there. He heard a door open.

"Come back here in a month. And don't eat so damned much. Trouble with you girls is you eat too damned much. Just makes it hard on me when the time comes."

Sandy heard Doc's gruff bark, followed by a muffled voice, a woman's voice, mumbling something in agreement as she and Doc walked down the hall to the waiting room. He chanced a peek and there, walking in the hall with Doc, was a woman he recognized. She seemed to be in a hurry, pulling her coat on over her dress, then passed out of his view in seconds. Even so, he knew immediately who she was just from her hair. He gaped...

Her auburn hair fell away from one side of her face and over her shoulder, setting off her pale blouse and making her bosom look particularly agreeable in Sandy's abbreviated view. As she walked she simultaneously straightened her skirt, held her purse, and clutched a handkerchief. She nodded as Doc growled at her to not drink alcohol and for damned sure to stay off her feet and get some help around the house. Sandy thought he heard her laugh at that, he wasn't sure why, and then he heard the door open to the waiting room. The lady was gone. He knew Doc would come back in to check his nose so he lay back down on the examining table and acted as if he were asleep to avoid being caught out at his spying.

Doc didn't come back.

Sandy waited. Doc's heavy steps clomped along the linoleum floor and passed the examining room without so much as a pause. He heard the man tread another dozen steps, go back into the room where he and the lady had been, and open the door.

Maybe he just forgot something. Like a thermometer. Or a shot. He hoped Doc hadn't forgotten a shot. He remembered the lock jaw shot Doc had jammed into him when he had cut his foot on the bean can lid. Nothing happened to his foot but his arm swelled up so big that his mother wanted to take him to Lubbock to a 'real doctor.' That made his nose itch and he began to pick at it, first to see if it was still bleeding but, after he started, because the scabs itched. Then he heard Doc's voice through the wall.

"Yeah. Get me Poppy on the line." A few moments passed, then Doc's voice boomed again. "Yeah, Poppy. Of course it's Doc Pritchard. How many other people named Doc are there in town? Did you think I was calling Bugs Bunny? Jesus."

Sandy waited while Poppy, whoever he was, answered the old coot.

"Of course I seen her." Pause. "Do I know what's wrong with her? Of course I know what's wrong with her. She's knocked up." Another pause. "How the hell would I know? I wasn't there."

Sandy had heard someone talk about being knocked up before, but he couldn't remember exactly who said it, or what it meant. He hadn't noticed the lady bleeding or anything like that so, whatever it meant, she must not have been hurt too much.

"Okay, so *Captain* Hastings was home on leave at Thanksgiving. That's when she got knocked up. What the hell does that leave? Mmm. December, January, February, ahh, whatever, August. August. That's when…" Pause. "Nah. Healthy as a horse." "I said a HORSE…" Pause. "No, I ain't been drinkin." The receiver slammed down with a clang, but Doc kept on muttering. "You're welcome, asshole. Keep an eye on her yourself."

When she had walked by the examining room door Sandy nearly forgot where he was. He couldn't think of her name but he knew her from the courthouse office where his mother went to sign up for ration books and coupons. *She's the most beautiful woman I've ever seen,* he thought. She wasn't very old, not much out of school. She was on the tall side and not too skinny, nor too fat, but just right. With her sharp facial lines and high forehead he thought she looked like a movie star or a princess or someone rich.

And Jeez, just look at that dark red hair! Now, while Doc was on the phone, Sandy wondered if she was sick or had broken something.

The next thing Sandy heard was a clank of glass, and he shuddered. That could only mean that Doc was fishing out one of those little medicine bottles with the rubber lids, and a big needle. He drew in his breath, then wiped his face to see if there was more blood on it. There wasn't. He wanted to jump off the examining table and run.

Instead, Doc's door opened again and Doc bulled his way down the hall. This time, without that woman to distract him, he glanced into the examining room and was startled to see Sandy on the table.

"What the hell are you doing here?"

"You told me to wait here."

"I didn't tell you to wait. I told you to keep your fingers clamped on your nose and quit fartin' around or I'd have to cut you open and sew you shut. The bleeding should've stopped a long time ago."

Despite his pronounced indifference Doc walked over to the table and pushed Sandy down on to his back, then grabbed his face with his thick hands and tilted it to get a better look up Sandy's nose. He used his bare fingers to claw out the blood-soaked cotton packing, which he flicked at a trash can.

"Hold still, you little fart. Let me look."

Sandy held still.

"I told you to stop fartin' around and you didn't. It started bleeding again. Damn."

Sandy was sure the bleeding started when Doc wrenched his head around and jerked out the gauze, but he was in no position to argue. Sure enough he tasted more blood going down his throat and felt, or thought he felt, a stream go down his face.

"Wait here. Don't move."

The doctor left, then returned. He laid something on the examining table, then packed more cotton gauze that had been soaked in something that stung enough to make Sandy jump. The fumes made him light headed. Doc again clamped Sandy's face in his hands, then began to wind a bandage with wet plaster across the boy's nose. The door opened. Sandy's mother came in.

"Doc! I ran as fast as I could. What happened? Is he…"

"He's all right. Tough kid. Just got hit in the face with some cow shit. Pardon me. Got hit in the face with something dirty. Still cleaning him up."

"What can I do?"

"Wait outside, that's what! Sterile environment. Don't want some germs gettin' in the kid while I'm closing him up. Just shut the door."

Sandy tried frantically to catch his mother's eyes but she hadn't come close enough and Doc's vice grip prevented him from moving his head side to side. He heard the door close, then the second door as his mother went out to the waiting room.

"Listen you little fart. Did you hear anything?"

Sandy tried to mumble that he had heard Doc say he was cleaning up Sandy's face, but that wasn't what Doc meant.

"Did you hear me on the telephone? No? Don't lie to me you little wart. I don't know what you heard or what you think you heard, but I'm gonna tell you right now you didn't hear a damned thing. Nothing. Understand?"

"MMPFH."

"Good. And you didn't see anybody in here either, did you. Got it? No one. I don't care if you did or not, but you damn well better care — you didn't! Got it?"

"MMPHF."

"Good. Now listen you little sneak. If I hear from anyone, anywhere, any time, one word of what happened in my office today, I'm going to have to look inside you again, because your nose is busted. And if I hear you talking about anybody being knocked up, or if I hear that you told someone that somebody is knocked up, I'm gonna cut your tonsils out and your voice box too and you'll never say another word to anybody because you won't have the squeak God gave a fucking tit mouse! Understand?"

When Doc turned loose of his face Sandy's eyes were as big as saucers. All he could feel was a huge bandage plastered over nearly everything that used to be between his eyes and his mouth, as if a papier maché coffee cup had been stuck on his nose.

"Answer me!"

"I uffersted."

"Good. Now get off of my table." Doc half helped, half shoved Sandy to the floor, then took him by the collar and marched him out to Mrs. Clayton in the waiting room.

"Doc? Is he going to be all right? What on earth happened?"

"Nothing. Boys'll be boys. Pokin' around where they shouldn't. He'll be all right. But he's got a busted nose. I'll have to repack it in a couple of days or a week. Bring him back. Fix him soup. No steaks. Ha, ha, ha."

She laughed, uncertainly, and assumed he meant it to be a joke about the meat rationing.

"If he's lucky it'll go back right. He's still growin'. But, if not, well, I'll have to break it again and straighten it. Keep the plaster clean and dry."

Mrs. Clayton nodded that she would. Sandy held her hand and, to her surprise, he seemed to be tugging on it to go.

"All right, that's all. And remember — I want to check up on him. Bring him back. And if he's got a problem with his nose, I'll fix it. Good-bye." He turned and left, slamming the waiting room door behind him.

"Well, young man, what do you have to say for yourself?"

He looked at his mother, pushed his way out to the sidewalk, and pulled on her hand to get her out of the clinic. She followed.

"Does it hurt? Well, no matter. I'll give you an aspirin. And if you have a problem, well, I'll just bring you back. Doc will take care of you."

That was exactly what Sandy was afraid of.

CHAPTER TWO

March, 1944

"You've got the fidgets. Here, take these potatoes out to the porch and peel them."

Mrs. Clayton handed him a paring knife and held open the screen door. Sandy took the pot of potatoes off the table, stepped out on to the back stoop, then sat down heavily to show his aggravation at being ordered to do even more chores.

"And put this down. Don't let the potatoes get on the porch. Or the peelings either." She handed a newspaper out through the screen door.

He spread the *Tierra Times* on the steps, then sat on the top one and began to peel. Every few moments he would cough, as quietly as he could, and clear his throat, then tone out 'La La La La La La La' the way he had seen Bugs Bunny and Elmer Fudd warming up for the opera. He had noticed since church Sunday that his voice squeaked up around ti and do. When he tried to hit the high notes his voice cracked. He felt his throat but nothing in particular seemed different there. Nevertheless, he was convinced that his tonsils would have to come out. He envisioned being taken into Pritchard's nasty little examining room, the grimy old cut-throat bending over him and prying his mouth open, Sandy's last spoken words being "I didn't tell anybody anything...," a futile protest before Doc clipped his vocal chords.

"What's going on out there?"

"Nothing."

"Have you got a cat out there?"

"No."

"Thought I heard something like a cat, except squeaky."

"Nope. Nothing here."

"Hurry up with the potatoes."

The wind gusted around the backyard, blowing the long green furls on the corn and flicking the leaves sprouting on the early tomatoes. He liked watching their victory garden come up. He had been given two rows, just his own, and he had picked out tomatoes and cucumbers. He hadn't known they were cucumbers — he had said pickles, but the bag of seeds clearly said cucumbers. There wasn't much going on with the cucumbers, but the tomatoes and his mother's corn were getting pretty tall. The wind whipped the newspaper sheets and Sandy glanced at the pages. He ignored the headlines, cotton prices, Japanese advances, to look for the comics. There weren't any. Giving in, he chose the first potato, turned it over, then around, then upside down, and began the slow process of scaling away the skin.

"All right, Mr. Tojo. Where are the secret bases? Eh? Won't talk? We'll see about that." He slipped the edge of the knife under the peel, then slowly, painstakingly, skinned off a third of Tojo's outer layer and dropped it on the newspaper.

"What kind of potatoes do you want?" his mother called through the screen door.

"French fries. With a steak."

He heard his mother laugh through the screen door.

She would bake them, he knew, but it would have been good to have French fries for a change. "Now will you tell me where the secret bases are? Not yet? Okay, take this." He deftly poked out three of Tojo's eyes with the point of the paring knife. "And this." He finished the potato, now half it's original size, dropped it on the newspaper, and picked up another. "So, Mr. Mussolini? Did you see what happened to your friend Tojo? Now will you tell me where you are hiding the submarine? No, we'll see about that." Mussolini lost half of his upper body. It dropped onto a section of the *Times* in which Poppy Sullivan had written that cattle prices would continue to rise unless FDR caused the market to crash after all the troops had been shipped overseas. Mussolini's arm pits and most of his back fell on the paragraph that said local cotton prices would go up, given the shortage after last November's fire at the cotton gin.

"Why can't we have French fries? And a steak? Mrs. Tarlton has steaks." He didn't expect his mother to answer; questions like these annoyed her, especially since his dad had gone off to work in Fort Worth. He wished his father was home more than a weekend every now and then.

"No ration coupons. No steaks." She called out through the screen door.

Sandy reached into the bowl and picked Hitler up, swiveling his nasty little body around, searching for the mustache.

An hour before, Sandy's mother had sent him off to get a haircut and bring home the mail. He liked the post office — there were posters on the bulletin board. He remembered the first time he had seen the B-24. It was glorious, four engines, two tails, and a bomb bay raining victory down on the Axis. He didn't know what a war bond was but if it would buy a B-24, Sandy wanted one. It was next to a fading instruction on how to plant a victory garden and a poster that Sluggo liked, kids playing in the sinister shadow of a swastika, a boy with a toy airplane, another with an American flag and a commodore's hat made from folded newspaper. Sandy's dad had taught him how to fold the newspaper into a cap.

Sandy had gone to look at the posters but there had been a crowd of people in front of the bulletin board and he couldn't squeeze his way to the front. He went instead to his mother's mail box, got down on his knees, and was trying to remember the combination when a cloying voice cooed down at him:

"Why Sandy Clayton — how's your nose? Oh goodness, that's quite a bandage."

He didn't even have to look up. It was like arsenic, sweet, or the gas chamber where the cyanide smells like almonds before it smothers you.

"Hello, Mrs. Tarlton," he answered.

"My, my, it looks like Dr. Pritchard put a wet paper bag on your nose. Oh, well, I guess he must know what's best. I'm surprised your mother lets you get out of the house."

"She sent me for the mail. And I'm supposed to get a haircut."

"A haircut? Did you say a haircut?"

"Yes, Ma'am."

"Well, no wonder, looking at your hair. I thought maybe you were a little girl at first." She giggled at her little joke; he wanted her to vanish into thin air and never return. "Well, that's just perfect. Since you're out, I do need for you to run a little errand for me. Just the littlest thing — please?"

Sandy suspected that despite her theatric sweetness Mrs. Tarlton was in league with Doc Pritchard. He was pretty sure that she was watching to see if he had said anything that Doc had told him not to say.

Mrs. Tarlton walked over to the wall of post office boxes, took out a key, and unlocked the biggest post office box he had ever seen, at least four times as large as his mother's. She withdrew a metal box from inside the postal box, opened a hinged lid, and took her mail out. Sandy had never seen such a big mail box as hers, so big that the three or four envelopes she took out seemed lost inside. He figured there was room for a hundred letters, if someone had that many. She put her mail in her coat pocket, felt around inside the box, then returned it to its place, closed the door, and locked it.

"Take this to Mr. Bradley. Please." She smiled with the lower half of her face, then held an envelope out and pushed it toward him. "Tell him that's all there was today. That's a good boy — now run."

He took the envelope from her. It didn't occur to him to say no. The barber shop was across the street from the post office and he had to go there anyway. He took Old Bradley's letter and went for his haircut.

The barber shop was different than anywhere else in Tierra. Old Bradley had a big swivel chair that he could raise or lower. A mirror on the back wall was lined with bottles of the colored stuff that Sandy had never seen Bradley use for anything. There was a jar like the one that held straws at the fountain over at the drug store, except this one had scissors and a straight razor, which he had seen the barber use on the men who came in for a shave. More than anything, though, Old Bradley was what made it different. The man was a talker. He remembered his last haircut:

"Hey, big boy. Hop in the chair. You been baptized yet?"

Sandy wasn't sure if this was a tale or a newly revealed streak of evangelism.

"Well, I was over at the church." Sandy knew this had to be a tale; Old Bradley never went to church. "Saw the preacher. He was back where they baptize people, you know, behind the place where he stands up and preaches. Anyways, he was takin' a bath. Soap and all. Naked. I'm serious, and I thought, why not? I suppose that's okay, if you don't mind being baptized in the preacher's bath water." Sandy wasn't sure it made any difference. "Course, most people pee in the bath water. Can't say about the preacher." That cracked Sandy up. It was the sort of thing he and Butch had talked about doing.

He liked Old Bradley's dog too, even if the mongrel was dirty and tried to lay down on you anytime you happened to be sitting on the sidewalk. He had tripped over it when he walked into the shop.

Butch claimed that there were pictures in Old Bradley's back room, where he kept the broom and the mop. Sometimes, Butch claimed, when the chair was swivelled just right, you could see pictures then. "They's naked. A bunch of 'em. The whole shebang. Everything!"

Butch lied about most things, even when the truth would have helped him, but Sandy suspected that he might be right about Old Bradley's broom closet. Every time he went in for a haircut he kept a lookout.

"Hey, big boy, what happened to you? Hop up in the chair."

"Aw, nothin'. Just a nosebleed."

"Looks like you got a paper bag stuck on your nose. Your mother want me to do anything different? A wet paper bag." Bradley stepped over to the counter by the mirror, picked up an electric clipper, studied the attachments, chose one, turned to his customer.

"Got a clod in the face. I'm all right."

"How'd you get a clod in the face?"

"Accident. We was throwin' clods the other day when the bombers came over."

"So one of the bombers dropped a clod on you?"

"Naw. It was one of *my* bombers. By the rules the battle was over, only one of the guys waited till I stood up and then threw a clod at me anyway."

Bradley just nodded, then applied the clippers to a matted knot on the corner of Sandy's head.

"It wasn't fair."

"What wasn't?

"Throwin' a clod after the battle was over. When the planes come, you win. It was a sneak attack."

"So who put the plaster on your face? Your mother didn't do it like that."

"Doc. Doc Pritchard."

"For a bloody nose? Why'd your mother take you to him? Must have been pretty bloody."

Sandy remembered the envelope.

"Stop squirming or you'll get a Mohawk."

That actually sounded pretty good. Sandy liked the idea of being the only guy with a Mohawk strip running from his forehead to his neck. The result would have been impressive, menacing.

"Here's this envelope. Sorry it's squashed. Mrs. Tarlton told me to bring it to you." He fished the envelope out and tried to smooth it, then handed it to Bradley out from under the drape. Bradley glanced at it, then put it in his pocket and continued cutting hair.

"Quit squirmin' around. Ain't nothing in that closet. So Mrs. Tarlton told you to bring this to me, eh? Did she open it?"

"Don't think so. I was down on my knees at my mom's box and she opened up this big old box and took it out, then told me to bring it to you."

"Okay. So where did this clod fight happen?"

"Aw, it was over by the tracks. Sluggo and I was us…"

"Whattaya mean, 'us?'"

"Americans. Us. And Butch and Tommy and Mike were the krauts. And we chased 'em over by the cotton shed and…"

"Need to keep away from that cotton shed. You'll get hurt there."

"Why? Ain't nothing but a door and a window and some burned walls."

"Roof'll fall in on you. I seen it happen before. Building catches fire, they put it out. Next thing you know somebody goes in there and the roof falls in on 'em. Hold still. I used to have this shop over in El Paso back when the Army was chasin' Pancho Villa back and forth. He'd show up at night and ride around stealin' cattle and horses, even guns. He'd come right across the Rio Grande and take whatever he wanted, ride back to Mexico. So they sent Old Black Jack to catch him. Old Black Jack couldn't have caught Pancho Villa with both hands and a bulldozer if they'd a tied him down with a rope and given him a sixty-second head start..."

Sandy had no idea who Pancho Villa was, or Black Jack either, but he liked the way Old Bradley told stories.

"... so one day Old Pancho comes over the river right in to El Paso and rides right up to the train and starts takin' stuff right out of the box cars. Someone calls Old Black Jack out at the fort and he comes ridin' up and starts shootin' at Old Pancho and Old Pancho gives him the finger, I swear to God, and rears his horse up and splashes back across the Rio Grande. Took everything he stole with him. I seen it with my own eyes. And so Old Black Jack takes a machine gun and shoots it off across the river and Old Pancho laughs and rides away, then comes back with a fucking cannon, 'scuse my French, and shoots back and it lands right on top of the train station and the next thing you know the damned thing is on fire. So they put the fire out and three days later two guys come in and I cut their hair. They say they work for the Southern Pacific. Well, I finish up and say good bye and they leave and go back to work and you know what happened? The roof of that old burned up train station falls in and killed them both."

"Golly."

"And I heard it was them two guys that had just been in and so I went to their funeral and you know what people said when they saw them there in the casket?"

"What?"

"'Look at their haircuts. Best I ever saw 'em look, almost like they was sleepin' they's so natural lookin'.' Get down. Tell your ma to stop by whenever it's convenient." Old Bradley put some powder on the back of Sandy's neck, brushed him off, and took the drape off with a toreador's flourish. Sandy got down.

"Anyways, stay away from that old cotton shed. You'll get hurt there. And stay away from Doc Pritchard, too. Ain't nobody goes there who's well and ain't nobody leaves there who ain't worse."

Sandy laughed. Old Bradley was pretty good at saying things like that. He wasn't worried about getting hurt at the burned out cotton gin; his dad had taken him there plenty of times before the fire. He did want to ask the barber what "knocked up" meant but was afraid to, partly from fear that it would get back to the doctor and partly from fear that Old Bradley might think a twelve-year-old who didn't know what "knocked up" meant must be pretty dumb. He decided not to talk about "knocked up," but he was sure old Bradley knew what it meant, that, and other things, too. Then he remembered.

"Butch says he's gonna be a pilot. What do you have to do to be a pilot?"

"Ain't but one way to fly planes and that's be an officer. Go to OCS. You guys ain't goin' to OCS. Soon's you're sixteen they'll draft you and send you straight to boot camp."

"What's OCS?"

"Officer's candidate school. Only way to get there is college. Draftees ain't goin' to college."

Sandy thought Butch might go to college. His dad owned the bank and his sister, Shirley, was a school teacher. He said as much to the barber.

"Maybe so." The way he said it sounded more like "not a chance." "Ain't sayin' nothing against the Flemings but I don't see the makings of an army captain, not in that house. Don't believe his dad was in the big one, the first war. He let the rest of us do his share of fightin' for him. Well, I don't know either way." He shook the hair out of the drape for emphasis, as if to say he did know but wasn't telling.

"So we won't be pilots, or even just ordinary captains? Like Captain Hastings?"

"Captain Hastings? Little Will? Well, guess he ain't so little now, forgot about him. Will Hastings ain't an army captain either, except he is."

"That doesn't make any sense. Who is Captain Hastings, anyway?"

"Little Will grew up here, high school anyways. Orphan. Real good kid. Went to school with Johnny. Was a blocker more'n a runner. Johnny, now, he is what you call a runnin' back. Fastest boy ever to come out of this town, and that's a fact. But Will — actually he wasn't much of a blocker, either, but a solid kid. Not real fast, but okay."

"Who's Johnny?"

"My boy. Him and Hoyt Carter run off to join the army right out of school. That was before they was draftin' anybody.' But not Will. He gets into college, don't know how, next thing you know I hear he's off to be a doctor."

"What's that got to do with being an officer?"

"They make army doctors into officers so they don't have to take orders from the privates and corporals lyin' there on the operating table. They tell a man 'I'm gonna cut your leg off,' the army doesn't want some soldier saying 'No, leave the leg and sew up this here splinter on my butt while you're at it.' So he's a medical doctor what the army drafted straight out of medical school. One day he's in med school, gets his sheepskin, then bang! Next day he's an officer in this man's army. No boot camp. No rifles or KP or none of that. Straight to captain and don't even learn 'em how to salute. Army takes every one of the kids out of medical school nowadays. Makes 'em an honorary gentleman, sends 'em off to plug holes in the real fightin' men. Ain't saying nothing against Will Hastings though, just he ain't a soldier. He's a doctor in a uniform. But a real doctor, not like that old coat hanger quack who uses Jack Daniels for rubbin' alcohol."

"Okay, Mr. Bradley. Thanks for the haircut. Mom said to put it on her account."

"Sure thing. See ya."

Butch was outside, waiting.

"Lemme see your nose. What'd Doc do — put a cast on your face?"

"Thanks for breaking my nose, dickhead. He told me to leave it alone or he'd have to operate. "

"Sorry. Hey, you didn't have to take that box of stuff to Old Lady Tarlton's."

Sandy didn't see the consolation in that. Butch was determined to make it sound like he had been the victim.

"She hands me this sorry box of groceries she had just bought at Reilly's and tells me to take it to her house. See this mutt here?" He pointed to Bradley's dog squirming in the dirt in front of the barber shop. "Well, about half way to her house I heard something back there and, sure enough, Old Bradley's dog was following me. Actually kind of nippin' on my tennis shoes.

"Hey, fella. Wanta go to a haunted house? Wanta see a spook?" Remember what's her name, the lady who married Count Alucard (Dracula spelled backwards)? Mrs. Tarlton looks just like her.

"Louise Albritton."

The dog had been interested in something more corporeal; Butch told how it began a series of jumps, each more aggressive than the last, snapping at the box of Mrs. Tarlton's groceries.

"I started trotting to keep that dog off her grocery box. Dog started trotting too. I ran, it ran. Time we got to Old Lady Tarlton's house the box was bouncing and the dog was jumping and I was kicking at it. Then I saw blood dripping out of the bottom of that box, and her door was locked. I was on her porch for twenty minutes kicking that dog off her supper. So she shows up and says 'Oh, Dearie, my oh my was the door locked? And why did you bring your dog?'"

"So she unlocks the door and I start to put the box down and it falls apart and blood gets on her table, so I picked the box back up but it was too late. Then Plop! Out pops this steak and it falls right on the floor, still bleeding all over the place. She was grabbing it and hiding it and there was blood everywhere. So what's wrong with your nose?"

"It's broken, you dunce."

"Hey, I didn't mean to break it. You shouldn't have stood up till we gave up."

"I wish it was *your* nose. Besides, I would have given her steak to the dog. I gotta go."

Sandy went back to the post office to get his mother's mail. He looked at the posters on the bulletin board and took a minute to read the draft board's newest announcement.

• •

'To all men age 18, or who will turn 18, NOTICE:

You must register for selective service on your 18th birthday. Your selective service office is located at 904 Broadway, Lubbock, Texas. Your local selective service board will meet in Room 114 of the Tierra County Court house on June 2, 1944. If you turned 18 years old after December 1, 1943, or have finished high school, left school, or are no longer employed in an essential war industry, you are to appear at that time for registration, medical fitness, and induction as directed by the board.

FAILURE TO APPEAR AND FAILURE TO REGISTER ARE FEDERAL CRIMES PUNISHABLE AS PROVIDED BY THE UNITED STATES CODE'

• •

The list on the left side of the bulletin board was still blank at the top, which meant that no one had been killed this month. The names on the bottom, wounded soldiers, were all boys from other towns, not from Tierra. Sandy didn't see anything that would have drawn the crowd that had gathered before Mrs. Tarlton had sent him off with Mr. Bradley's mail. He got down on his knees in front of his parent's box and began to dial in the combination. *Turn three times to the right and stop on J. Turn twice to the left and stop on F. Turn once to the right and stop on B. Or is it twice to the right and stop on A?*

"Bart! Come out here!"

Sandy heard a woman's voice, a very angry voice, barking at someone. Sandy looked up and saw two legs extending behind the partition that separated the post office clerk's window from the wall where the mail boxes were lined up. They were nice legs as far as it went, although the shoes weren't much.

"Why, hello, Sis. What's on your mind?"

Sandy was pretty sure it was the postmaster, partially because he was the only possible man in the place and partially because the guys all referred to the postmaster as "Bart the Fart." They thought Bart was a draft dodger.

"Give me my mail, Bart. Give it to me. Now." Her voice sounded controlled but even Sandy could hear the anger.

"Why sure, Sis. Just wait there. Glad to know it was yours."

"You knew very well that letter was mine before you tacked it up on the bulletin board for the whole town to read. Don't play innocent with me..."

Sandy wasn't sure what she was going to call Bart because her voice trailed off. He looked up to see the postmaster hand over a letter to the woman at the counter, then ducked back down and began to root around in the mail box, trying not to be noticed. He wasn't.

"Miss Somerville called from the telephone exchange. She said you put up one of my letters on the bulletin board and I better get over here because everybody in town was standing here reading it."

"It wasn't *addressed* to you, Gin. I couldn't truthfully say who it was addressed to. The envelope was all marked up, just the name of the town. I could have just thrown it away — instead, I did the good thing — I put it up to see if anybody knew who it was for...."

"Oh, yes, by all means. Let me see, Bart — says right here on the first line 'Dear Virginia.' Are there a lot of people in Tierra who receive V–Mail that begins 'Dear Virginia?' And when you turn it over, and look at the address, it says 'Hastings, such and such battalion, England.' Is it hard in your job to locate people who get army mail from Hastingses in England? Why, you must find your job to be very difficult, Bart. How did you get your job, anyway?"

"It could have been from anybody named Hastings. How many Hastings are there in the Army? It doesn't have to be your Hastings. Why couldn't one of those other Hastings write somebody here? And if it was from Will, so what? He knows everybody in town. He might be writing to somebody besides you. In fact, you might be surprised at what I see come through the mail."

Sandy heard a resounding "thwack." He knew that the woman had slapped Bart Sullivan as hard as she could. He glanced up to see her spin on her feet and walk out of the post office, clutching an opened army letter in her right hand. He knew it was an army letter because he had seen them at Mr. Bradley's before.

Sandy heard Bart snort out a final retort at the closed door but he still counted to ten before getting up from his mother's mail box. The only mail was bills, from the electric company, the phone company, the *Tierra Times*, but nothing from Fort Worth. He peered at the window where Bart would be if he was still there staring out the door. Sandy saw no one and slipped out.

He looked toward the square. The lady was on the sidewalk, hurrying in the direction of the courthouse. Sandy thought about running after her, to remind her that Doc had told her to keep off her feet, then realized that if he told her that he would find himself stretched out on one of Doc's tables faster than he could say "Cock Robin." He slowed to a walk, then turned around and headed back home.

He had been gone an hour but his mother hadn't said anything when he gave her the mail. He thought about telling her what Mr. Bradley said, that he would have to go to college if he was going to fly airplanes, but she was busy so he just let it go. First she had sent him out to hang the wash on the clothes line; now he was peeling potatoes on the back porch.

"Mrs. Tarlton has steak. Why can't we?"

"Because she must have enough ration stamps. We don't have ration stamps for steaks. So, how about French fries and there's still some chicken from last night. Does that sound good?"

"How come she has stamps and we don't?"

"Wish I knew. You about through out there?"

"Yes, ma'am."

Sandy took Hitler by the neck, poked at his eyes with his bayonet, then peeled his uniform away. *I'd rather have a steak*, he thought, *especially if all it takes is getting some ration stamps. Butch said he saw a whole bowl of 'em on Mrs. Tarlton's hall table.* And this time he believed Butch; after all, she did have a steak, and butter too.

"You're awful quiet out there."

He was thinking. The letters he had seen in the barber shop on Old Bradley's mirror were Army letters like the Army letter the lady got at the post office. Johnny Bradley and Captain Hastings were in the army. There was rationing because the army needed the steaks and everything else to fight the war. If Miss Sullivan and Old Bradley could do without because of the war, he should do without, too. Sandy also thought he had figured out what "knocked up" meant, and why she was supposed to keep off her feet and let somebody else help out around the house: Captain Hastings had been home last Thanksgiving. *At least he wasn't doing without...*

Sandy smiled when he figured out this last connection, then made a few final stabs at Hitler's mustache and dropped the dismembered dictator into the pot with the other potatoes.

CHAPTER THREE

❧

April 1944

If Sandy had read the *Tierra Times* he might have figured out that he had no further need to fear Doc Pritchard. On the Sunday before Easter, between the story about the community egg hunt on the courthouse lawn and a column which began and ended with a list of Easter Services, there was an announcement:

> Mr. Michael Sullivan wishes to announce that his daughter, Virginia Sullivan, of Tierra, and Captain Woodrow Wilson Hastings, a graduate of Tierra High School and the University of Texas Medical School at Galveston and now of the United States Army in Europe, entered into the holy state of matrimony before a justice of the peace in Clovis, New Mexico during his leave over the Thanksgiving Holiday, November 25, 1943.

There was a ribbon and heart beneath the announcement.

Michael Sullivan, Poppy, *was* the *Tierra Times*. He had taken Doc Pritchard's phone call, then thought through the implications of his pregnant daughter and her soldier/doctor five thousand miles away in England. He decided it was a good thing and made several decisions about the couple's, and the town's, future. Two weeks later he published his announcement of their elopement, an imaginary union that was as much a surprise to his daughter as to the rest of the community.

Sandy may not have read the announcement but everyone else did. Regardless of what might have been said at the beauty shop, the town congratulated Poppy and wished the happy couple well. Mrs. Tarlton and Shirley's mother, with visions of missed cakes and needlework dresses, clucked over the lost opportunity to stage a wedding, but their seed fell on thin soil. Others, keenly aware of Poppy Sullivan's encyclopedic knowledge of local wealth — who had spare blue ration coupons, a tire hidden in a loft, a cattle pen with more yearlings than reported to the OPA contractor, a farmer with one tractor and gasoline tanks for three — breathed a sigh of relief that no gifts were called for, at least not yet. For Poppy, it was business as usual. He composed the next edition of the *Times*, stopped in at the bank and the co-op to talk about cotton prices, and kept an eye on Bart's urges.

The two who didn't congratulate Poppy on his announcement were Virginia herself and Butch's sister Shirley.

Virginia had learned of her marriage to Will the same way she learned most things about their long-distance courtship — she read it when Bart tacked it to the bulletin board at the post office. Her first reaction had been disbelief. She pulled out the thumbtack and the wedding announcement, looked around the room to see who was watching, and stormed out. By the time she got to the newspaper office, disbelief had turned to fury.

Her fury fell on deaf ears.

"What's done is done," Poppy told her. "You did what you had to do so I did what I had to do. You'd better learn to live with it — like I tell Bart, take the long view."

"How dare you…?"

"How dare I what? You are hereby married to Will. The paper says so. But," and he paused long enough for her to recognize the familiar sign of Poppy's threats, "if you want to go tell everyone in town that it was a misprint, well that'll give them two things to talk about when you start to show. What's done is done."

He let the warning sink in. Who would people believe? Her or Poppy? And their own eyes. "And besides — you couldn't have made me happier! When Will comes home, well —" He waxed poetic at the thought of Will coming home to become the town's beloved doctor. "He'll build you a two-story home. There'll be more babies, nice cars, maybe even a real hospital. He'll be the man everyone wants, school boards, the bank, the cotton co-op." Will, and Virginia, would reflect in the glow of Poppy's golden years and Tierra would be eternally grateful. "I suggest that you give these people what they want — a war bride. When God gives you crumbs, go bake a cake. A wedding cake."

For the next two hours Virginia sat at her desk in the courthouse, her eyes fixed on ration coupon books, OPA registries, and bulletins announcing rules changes in the number of yellow coupons that could be used to supplement red stamps for meat (not very many) or blue stamps for cottage cheese (no limit). Her mind, however, was not focused on month-to-month whimsies of the Office of Price Administration.

From the moment Doc Pritchard had told her to get dressed, Virginia had imagined the day when she would tell Poppy she was pregnant. His reaction would be to slap her (possibly), to insult her for sleeping around (probably), to ask how she thought it would make him look in the eyes of the town (certainly), and to tell Bart that Virginia, too, had brought shame on the family (as he had done when they left Emma at the State Hospital in Lubbock). She would stand defiant. If he slapped her, she would smile. To his accusation, she would tell the truth: she had not slept around. *He's the only one, and I planned it as much as he did. Maybe more.* As for how it would make Poppy look, Virginia carefully scripted the scene: *For once, Poppy, it isn't about you! It is my baby and I'll have it no matter what you or anyone in town says!* As for Bart, she would snort that at least one of Poppy's children could procreate. She had no answer if Poppy were to say anything hateful about her mother; she prayed he would not.

Nothing she had planned for had come to pass. She was flabbergasted that he had announced in the *Times* that she had eloped with Will. He might have expected her to elope to defuse an embarrassing pregnancy, but he wasn't embarrassed — he was delighted! *He should hate me; instead he's turning it into another opportunity to own the town...* She thought of how often she had seriously considered marrying Will (a few times, not many) and of how often Poppy succeeded in making her do as he wished (every time). To those thoughts she added a fair degree of anxiety, given that she was likely to lose her job at the ration desk when the county commissioners learned that she was pregnant and a war bride to boot, a woman whose husband who could send money home from the army.

And, to her credit, she was concerned for Will. What would he think when someone told him that he was married to the girl who, the last time she saw him, had not agreed to wait for him? She hadn't been prepared to marry him but she also hadn't set out to hurt him.

By five o'clock she had cooled off. She left the courthouse, marched down the wooden sidewalk past the general store and the bank, and stopped in at the drug store before circling back to Reilly's Grocery. She knew it never occurred to Poppy to ask his daughter's permission to announce her elopement to cover up her pregnancy. Even so, as anger and uncertainty wrestled for primacy, she understood why Poppy had done it. Every single person in Tierra depended on him one way or another. He was looked to and listened to, his help sought by all. Now his daughter was pregnant and her soldier was five thousand miles away. Poppy could not lose face before the town. It was then that Virginia saw Shirley Fleming walk out the front door of Reilly's Grocery.

"Hello, Shirley."

Virginia saw Shirley's eyes bulge and her face tighten. *She knows.* It was the first joy Virginia experienced as a married woman. She actually smiled.

"Hello, Virginia." Shirley quickly put up her own guard, tilting her head to the right and peering at Virginia from the left sides of her eyes, arching her brows in rebuke, as if Virginia was one of her third grade pupils. She crossed her arms and made no secret of examining Virginia from head to toe for evidence of a shotgun to explain the surprise wedding announcement. "Congratulations," she resumed, "Will must be very…happy."

"He certainly is," Virginia answered. "He always wanted to get married. Of course, you know that. When was the first time he proposed to me? Let me think."

They both knew the first time. It had been at their high school graduation dance, one week after Will had told Virginia that he had a scholarship. Will had broken up with Shirley at the football Homecoming Dance and Shirley had accused him, correctly, of wanting to "go out" with Virginia. Virginia indeed had wanted to go out with Will; he was rather nice to look at and reasonably intelligent and, as much as anything else, Shirley had him. For the rest of their senior year merely going out with Will had been pleasant enough. He had bought her a record for Christmas, some chocolate on Valentine's Day, and a corsage at Easter. When Spring rains had filled the quarry, they went swimming with Hoyt and Johnny and Molly, although not with Shirley and definitely not with Bart. And, of course, she and Will had gone to the quarry by themselves, once, ostensibly to swim. Even now Virginia enjoyed the memory of their senior year.

Then came the graduation dance. The first shock had been that Hoyt Carter and Johnny Bradley had signed up for the army. "Got nowhere else to work, not here," they had said. "We *have* to go to the army."

The second shock had been Will's college scholarship. "Just got this letter," he had said, showing her. "And if I do well the first two years, they'll let me go to medical school." The letter did say that. At eighteen she was not sufficiently experienced to consider that such a scholarship was quite unusual, mysterious even.

"I'll have a future, Virginia, a real future. Will you…?"

At that first of many proposals, Virginia had said no. She wasn't ready to settle down, something Will should have figured out for himself from the incident at the quarry. Rumors, never proved, also held that Shirley had proposed to Will, who likewise said no. It was no secret, however, that Virginia suggested to Shirley that she encourage Hoyt Carter, an act Virginia regretted because of the scorn it brought to Hoyt from the cheerleader who said he wasn't good enough.

And thus ensued the first of many parting scenes at the Greyhound bus stop in front of Nona's Café. Hoyt tried to say goodbye to Shirley, who ignored him. Molly said goodbye to Johnny, then burst into tears. Bart, at a distance, said good riddance to all of them, to Molly who deserved it for picking Johnny over Bart and to Shirley who had chosen Will over Bart. He had gotten even with Johnny, and Hoyt in the bargain, but in his mind he still had a score to settle with Will. As oblivious to Bart as to Hoyt, Shirley spied. Will asked Virginia to "wait for him," which Virginia thought was sweet but, knowing instinctively what happened to girls who waited for boys away at college, she didn't exactly promise she would. The bus pulled away. The Flemings drove Shirley off to college at Texas Tech. Virginia assumed that she had probably seen the last of all of them.

Virginia would have written Will a letter to finish it herself except that, at Christmas, Shirley had come home from school and made the mistake of letting it be known that she had been writing from her dormitory room in Lubbock to Will at his in El Paso. That was enough to make Virginia decide to re-kindle Will's flame. At the end of Christmas he stood on the bus steps and asked her again. Everyone in town knew it.

When he came home for summer, that year and every summer and holiday afterward, Shirley beat Virginia to the bus stop. Hers was the first face Will saw. In September, then and every year after, when it was time for Will to go back to school or to summer internships or Will's first military training after medical school, Shirley showed up at the bus stop and stood by as Will again asked Virginia to wait for him. At first Virginia would have broken it off if Shirley hadn't been so stupid as to keep showing up, and showing interest, at times when Virginia had the expectation of enough privacy to tell Will it was over. However, as they went along, Virginia was less sure. The nice looking boy gradually became a thoughtful and caring, albeit quiet, young man. Will's boyish good looks matured into a kind face and gentle demeanor. If anything, he was even more tolerable to look at and very well educated, at least compared to anyone else Virginia knew. More than once, she almost agreed to wait for him. This went on among the three of them for seven years.

"Well, no matter, Shirley. That's all history now, isn't it?" It was not so clear that Virginia really wanted her prize as much as the consolation of knowing that Shirley had lost hers. "We can all stop wondering about it now, can't we?"

"I was just so — what is the word?" Furious was the word, but even Shirley couldn't say that. "Surprised? Yes, surprised. That's the word. And here we are, let's see, December, January, February, March, April. Yes, here we are in April and your little secret comes out, doesn't it? I'm — surprised — that you didn't announce it at Thanksgiving. Why, bless your little heart, we could have had a party before Will had to go off, couldn't we?"

"Well, you know me, Shirley. I never do things the easy way."

Virginia also knew that Shirley knew that in Thanksgiving, before he shipped out, Will had asked Virginia one more time. Shirley had been there at the bus stop when Will and his brother left on the bus. The routine had not changed: Will had been polite to Shirley, waved goodbye to whomever was there, and humped his barracks bag into the baggage well of the bus. He then had embraced Virginia and asked her to wait for him. Virginia had smiled, given him a brief kiss and a hug, promised nothing, and waved goodbye as the bus pulled away, leaving him hanging, just as she always had done. The bus disappeared, as it always did. To Shirley, Virginia had appeared to suffer no more pains of separation from Will than she usually did and was quietly relieved that she still had a chance. Shirley had suffered in silence. As she always did.

It didn't take a third grade teacher to wonder in April why in November the last words from someone who had just eloped would be *will you wait for me?* Shirley smelled the rat.

"And what does Will say? I can just imagine our little married soldier — waking up to find out that he's in the army and has a wife back home. My, my."

"Will is fine, as cold and wet and as miserable as everybody else. Married or single."

"Well, I sure hope he's looking out for himself. There's no telling what kind of trouble he might find himself in." She paused for a moment to let the effect sink in, then equivocated. "This field surgeon business."

Virginia wondered whether Shirley might be holding out an olive branch now that Will was hopelessly beyond her reach. She wasn't.

"And Will's brother? Peter?" She continued. "What do you hear from Peter?"

Virginia had to catch her breath. She had been as surprised as anyone when Will told her he had a brother and that he had invited him home for Thanksgiving before Will was to ship out. "I told him I wanted him to meet my girl and see my town," Will had told her.

He was something. Rather than looking a year or two older, Peter was so much like Will that he could have been his twin, except Peter was loudly infectious where Will was quiet, quick where Will was thoughtful. Peter dared to sneak a drop of cheer after the parents went to bed, then took them out to swing dance in the street to the music of a car radio. He told outrageous stories of glider planes flying through open hangars and of buddies extracted from barracks windows to go jitterbug at the Aviatrix Club a hundred yards from the air base gate. Will loved him without limit or question, and it was easy to do.

Shirley had tagged along everywhere, to dinner, to dance, to drink weak coffee at Nona's and listen to army stories. Peter had gotten on the bus with Will. Shirley couldn't be trusted with the church silver but maybe, just maybe, she had given up on Will. Maybe Shirley had an eye for Peter. Virginia's better instincts took charge.

"Peter? I haven't heard a word. Not lately. Will hasn't said a thing," a true answer as far as it went.

"Well, bless your heart, Virginia, I'm sure you'll make Will—" *Miserable*, she thought. She let the phrase hang in the air, then stepped around the newlywed bride and walked away.

"Hello, Mr. Reilly."

"Ah, Virginia, hello. How is our little bride? Congratulations."

"Yes, thanks. But I still have to cook dinner for Poppy." *And Bart.*

"But this is such a special day. We were so pleased when we read the announcement. Weren't we, Dear?" Reilly turned to Mrs. Reilly, at the cash register, glowing over the joy the Reillys had felt when they read about Poppy's daughter. Mrs. Reilly concurred. "A special day. Is there any little thing I can get for you? Something to brighten the table?" He winked to let her know that he might be able to find a few tidbits that weren't necessarily on the shelf, a grocer's secret shared by almost everyone in Tierra.

"Why yes, Mr. Reilly, there is something. Just a few potatoes — you know Poppy. And if you have a little piece of pork or some ground meat — Bart won't be too particular, whatever we have room for in the ration book."

"Of course, of course, no problem."

"But I would like to make them a cake."

That slowed Reilly down. Real cakes, with flour, baking powder and soda, sugar, butter, no one could get together enough ingredients and coupons to make more than one a year, and that required months of saving.

"Let me look, Dear. Mrs. Reilly may have a bit of sugar set aside. For us. If she does, it's yours."

"Oh, don't worry about the sugar, Mr. Reilly. The ladies at church said to use molasses; I think we have plenty."

"Fine. Perfect." Reilly breathed a little easier, his fears that Virginia was as selfish as Bart eased. "A nice white cake, Dear. Let me see what we need…"

Virginia didn't correct him. Instead, she began to read the list of ingredients.

"White flour. I need at least two cups."

"Oh, dear. Mrs. Reilly stretches her flour with bread crumbs. Do you think…."

"That'll be just fine, as long as it adds up to two cups. Sugar. We've covered that. In fact, molasses is better for the cake I have in mind. Eggs."

"Don't ask. Just look in your box when you get home." He winked. There were so many chickens in Tierra, around Tierra, and walking freely around the streets of Tierra that the OPA buyers didn't even attempt to enforce the egg ration. "What else?"

"Butter."

Mr. Reilly hated to hear this. What the government men conceded on the poultry front they made up for in butter vigilance. On the other hand, helping Virginia bake a special cake for Poppy was a challenge and, he worried, a test. If anyone could spot the difference between butter and margarine, it was Poppy. He considered suggesting half butter, half apple-sauce, but gave in.

"You tell Poppy I said this is a special cake. Let me see if I can find some butter. There may be a smidgen...."

"Milk."

"Milk. Hmm." Despite the government clamp on butter, even in Tierra, milk was so easy to cheat that Reilly was suspicious — most people bought it right out of the can at the Cochran's dairy just north of town. It never occurred to him that the Sullivans were indifferent to milk. But, if it was a test....

"And pecans? Do you have any pecans? I know they're out of season, but ..."

Mr. Reilly resigned himself to breaking into his most secret stores. Virginia seemed to know what was hidden in the back; he assumed that Poppy had told his children everything that he had scrounged for Reilly over the difficult war months. Thus, in short order, he unearthed necessary extracts, ground spices, salt, soda, and powders.

Virginia turned to the equally difficult chore of picking a few decent potatoes to go with whatever Reilly would part with, be it a hidden pork loin or even some hammered cutlets. She really didn't care. In fact, she preferred that neither Bart nor her father enjoy dinner too much; she wanted them hungry for cake.

She was halfway through Reilly's potato bin before the rest of Shirley's comment registered on her. *How does she know Will is in field surgeon school? I didn't say anything about it, not to her and not to anyone else.* She dropped her bag of potatoes and wheeled around to make for the front door. *There's only one place Shirley could have learned that. It's time for me to put some stamps on the postmaster....* In doing so, she knocked into Sandy, who stumbled and fell to the wood plank floor, then tried to pick up her potatoes before they rolled as far as Reilly's pickle and cracker aisle. Virginia bumped up against the potato bin to keep from falling herself.

"Whoops!!! Hey, Sweetie — what are you doing under my feet?" There was a sheepish and rather cute boy curled up on the floor, picking up her potatoes. She tried to remember his name.

"Sorry. I just saw your potatoes, I mean, saw you dropping things, and I,..." He looked up at her, reasonably sure that he should not tell her he had followed her around after he saw her come in the store. He picked up the potatoes and stood up, trying to hand them to her.

For her part, she was trying to step around him in order to go to the post office to assault her brother. For his part, Sandy stepped right when she stepped left, then to his left to her right, and generally got in her way.

"For God sake, what did you do to your nose? It's bleeding."

He reached up to wipe it with his sleeve.

"Don't do that. Here." She reached into her handbag for a handkerchief, drew it out and handed it to him. "Put this to your nose. What happened?"

"I got it busted. A couple of weeks ago." He didn't tell her that she had kicked him in the face when he went down on the floor for her groceries. "It'll be all right."

"Hold your head back. Stand there."

He stood with his head tilted and his back against the vegetable bin, his right hand juggling Virginia's potatoes, his left hand packing her handkerchief against his nose. She came back with Mr. Reilly and a glass of water.

"Dampen the hanky. Now, put it in your nose. Did I kick you?"

"No, Ma'am. I think it's already stopped bleeding. It'll be all right. I just got the plaster off of it Saturday and it still bleeds pretty easy. Hope I didn't mess up your hanky."

"Are you the boy who got hit in the face with cow... er, over by the cattle chutes?"

Sandy was mortified that Virginia knew about his nose.

"It'll be all right. I'll be fine, for sure."

"What's going on?" Reilly chimed in. "Sandy, stand back — don't bleed on the vegetables." His nose was menacing the turnips and onions. "Pick Miss Sullivan's bag up. Miss Sullivan! Listen to me; I have to learn to say Mrs. Hastings. Pick Mrs. Hastings' bag up and take it to the register. And don't bleed in it. Sandy's helping out, Virginia. Or do you prefer I say Mrs. Hastings?" He wiped his hands on his apron and rocked a bit on his heels and toes.

She didn't say.

"Sandy comes by after school now, to sweep up a bit, help the ladies carry their groceries home, that sort of thing. I'm trying to do my bit, too, even if it's just to help the Claytons." He drew closer to her and continued. "Sandy's dad is in Fort Worth. At the Consolidated plant. I guess you probably knew that. Shame that the cotton gin burned down. Seems like if we don't lose the boys to the army we lose 'em to war work. Guess you know that better than anybody."

Reilly did feel as bad as everyone else about the cotton gin. The *Times* had written that the men were going to start work "any day" to tear down the burned-out wreck and get the new one built before the first cotton picking. Until then there would be no job for most of the men who had worked at the Co-op before the fire, Sandy's dad included. "Let me get Sandy to carry your groceries home, Virginia. That's what he's for."

By this time Virginia's plan to assault Bart had simmered. Tierra had tittered for years about Shirley wanting Will, Will wanting Virginia, and Virginia keeping them both just out of reach. Now she was supposedly married to him, at least as far as Tierra was concerned, and there wasn't anything she could do about it until after the war. To publicly accuse Bart of letting Shirley read Will's letters would fuel more gossip. She slowed down enough to admit that it wasn't a good idea to storm over to the post office and let Bart give the town something new to talk about. Her phantom wedding and soon, the inevitable display of a swelling abdomen, were going to be difficult enough without Mrs. Tarlton whispering about a love triangle. She would find out what Shirley knew another way, another time.

Fifteen minutes later Sandy found himself carrying a box of groceries and walking alongside his mystery woman, head held high to ward off another nosebleed. Virginia had to warn him to watch his step at the edge of the sidewalk, again as they walked across the roots of the oak trees on the courthouse lawn, and a third time when they stepped off the curb at the truck entrance to Franklin's Hardware and Supply. He banged his shins struggling up the steps of the Sullivan home three blocks away, thus releasing the giggle she had suppressed every time the boy had juggled her box, grabbed at sacks and bottles, and stumbled his way up the steps. Her laugh finally erupted when they got into the kitchen and he set the groceries down. She saw him eye the contents of the grocery box.

"Do we eat a lot of coconut? Why, no, Sandy, I don't believe we do eat a lot of coconut. Do you eat a lot of coconut?"

"Well, no Ma'am. In fact, I don't think I ever ate coconut before. But I couldn't help seeing you had a can of coconut and I thought...." He thought perhaps it was a women's secret, that pregnant women craved certain foods, like pickles. Coconut could be one of them.

"No, Sandy, we don't either. But today's a special occasion and I need some coconut. Mr. Reilly had a can that he'd been holding back. He let me have it."

Sandy couldn't imagine how coconut got into cans, much less why Mr. Reilly would have one or would hold one back.

"Yes, today is a special day, so I'm going to bake a cake. And, to do that, I need coconut. And pecans, too."

"I know how to shell pecans, Mrs. Hastings, I really do. You take a hammer, tap 'em a bit, then when they fall apart, you dig out the pecan. Do you want me to shell some pecans for you?"

"How long have you been working for Mr. Reilly?"

"Just a couple of days. He let me start Monday. I'm trying to get something for Dad. He'll come home for his birthday. But I don't have any money."

"When's his birthday?"

"June. June 6. About two weeks after school lets out. It's a week before mine."

"How much money are you trying to earn?"

Sandy didn't tell her, partly because he was embarrassed and partly because he didn't know. He wanted to buy his father a new car so he could come home more often. His mother had laughed at the idea. "There aren't any new cars, Dear, not even any old ones. No one has had a car to sell since the war started. In fact, no one even has tires, or gasoline." But Sandy was going to try.

"You need to get on back to Reilly's. He pays you and I'm afraid I can't pay you to shell pecans." It occurred to her that maybe she was supposed to pay him, a tip at least. She wondered if she had any change. "Can you wait here a minute?" She left and went to her bedroom to see if there was a dime or a couple of nickels on the dresser that she could give him as a tip.

Sandy looked around. He had been by the Sullivan house a hundred times, on his bicycle, flying newspaper kites, chasing a dog, advancing or retreating with the armies. There were only a thousand or twelve hundred people in Tierra, no house much different from any other. The Sullivan kitchen, though, seemed different than his mother's kitchen. There were dirty dishes in the sink and bread was lying open on the counter. A toaster, next to the cook top, was sprung open and the crumbs were piling up on the counter. The waste basket was beside the table, egg crumbs and apple peels plonked on top like someone had just leaned over from the breakfast table to scrape their plate clean. Sandy's mother kept a spotless kitchen. Her scraps went straight into the garden and the trash was out of sight. Sandy liked the smell of the Sullivan kitchen, though, an aroma of fried foods and something indistinct, sweet but in a sickly way, perhaps in the ice box.

He wondered whether she had a picture of Captain Hastings in the living room, maybe on the radio or the lamp table. He had an idea of what a Captain Hastings should look like, even if he was a doctor/captain rather than a pilot or a real soldier. For a woman like her, hair all pulled back on one side and cascading down over her shoulder on the other side like she had turned around just to look at you, and *the rest of her*, as he said to himself, Sandy had concluded that for her it would take a special man. He had imagined someone no less than six feet two inches tall with broad shoulders, a square jaw, and dark hair. In fact, he expected Will Hastings to look exactly like Johnny Mack Brown, the Ghost Rider, except in a uniform. There was no picture on the radio or the lamp table and he slipped back into the kitchen.

"Sandy, here, thank you for carrying the groceries home." She gave him the only nickel she could find.

He didn't want to accept it, even though it had been Mrs. Tarlton's giving a dime to Butch Fleming the day Sandy's nose was broken that had given him the idea to carry groceries at Reilly's in the first place.

"Naw, Ma'am. I didn't do it for pay."

"No, here, you take it, and thank you."

"Yes Ma'am. Say, would you like me to come back and shell your pecans? I'd be happy to do it. Wouldn't charge you, just help out."

"Why, that's very nice Sandy, but no, you don't have to do that. But thank you."

"How many pecans do you need? I could take 'em home myself and bring 'em back."

For the first time she actually looked at Sandy and realized that the boy was smitten. *What else could possibly happen to me today?* She knew the right thing to do was politely decline, then let him come back after work and shell her pecans. The difficulty was that, even if it was the one nice thing that happened in a day of bad things, she didn't want a smitten boy; she just wanted to be alone. The roller coaster was down again and she wanted to get off, at least long enough to rest and think what to do.

"No, Sandy. Go on back to Mr. Reilly's. This time I'll do it myself. But thank you. Run along."

Besides, she thought, and smiled to herself, *I have a cake to bake.*

Sandy was certain that he had made an idiot of himself. Even so, it was plain that neither Mrs. Hastings nor Bart the Fart nor anyone else had done much around the house in a long time. There was no victory garden. The little patch of grass behind the Sullivan home had not been cut. Their well house was littered with piles of scrap lumber, some screens, chicken wire and debris of various kinds. He wandered around the side of the house, then across the backyard and under the sagging clothes line before skipping over to the street to walk back to Reilly's.

Well, Doc told her to get some help around the house. I can do it on Sundays, when the grocery store is closed.

Virginia turned back to Emma's scrapbook of recipes and ingredients, found "white cake," and re-checked. Sure enough, the ingredients were exactly the same for plain chocolate cake, except for the chocolate.

A substitute for chocolate? No problem. I have just the thing. She began to sift, measure, and stir. At the step when she should have added chocolate, she poured in a half-bottle of Dr. Castor's Black Draft Laxative. *For children —
stir with molasses for a taste like cocoa.* It wasn't true but, taken with enough

molasses, it would be hard to taste the difference, and the color was just right. *If Bart has any guts, a castor oil molasses chocolate cake ought to take care of them.* And, as everyone kept saying, it couldn't be helped — it was the war.

It was while she stirred the ingredients together that Virginia admitted how badly she missed her mother, and began to cry.

CHAPTER FOUR

May, 1944

By Saturday evening Sandy had earned less than two dollars. He counted the weeks until his father's birthday and concluded that saving enough to buy a car might take longer than he expected, by three or four years. He put his earnings into a Mason jar, screwed the lid off, removed 3 pennies, screwed the lid on, and asked permission to go play with Butch and Sluggo. They met at the gate by Franklin's lumber yard.

"Let's go up in the two-by-fours and set up a fort."

"Naw. Mr. Franklin told my dad he'd caught us up there again. He said next time he'd give me a whippin.'"

"It's Saturday. Who'd tell him?" Butch wasn't too troubled about Sluggo getting in trouble. Not too many people in Tierra complained about the banker's son.

"Let's go hit flies."

"Got your ball?"

"I can go get it. Got your bat?"

"I can go get it." None of them had a glove.

They met in the vacant lot between Nona's Café and Homer's Magnolia Station. The cotton fields beyond the railroad tracks on the other side of the highway were lined in straight rows, their green leaves giving the scrubby farm land a green veneer, the promise of a bumper crop that could offset the huge loss of bales inside the gin at the time of the fire. The Co-op office and the train depot, between the highway and the train track, were the only buildings on the south side of the road, not counting the burned out shell of the cotton gin. Collectively, they gave Tierra an air of having been abandoned.

Butch not only owned the bat, he was the better hitter. Sluggo was the worst batter but could throw the ball reasonably close to home plate, a scrap of tin from the cotton gin. That put Sandy in the outfield, delineated by Nona's Café, the Magnolia Station, and the Clovis Highway.

Whack! Butch hit a grounder to Sluggo, who jumped to avoid being hit in the shins. Whack. Another grounder, this time to the left and off a rock. Sluggo tripped in a prairie dog hole and landed in a sticker patch.

"Hey. You're supposed to hit flies! Jesus!" Butch could hit flies but the rule was that once a fly was caught they rotated. He preferred batting to being in the outfield and so prolonged his turn at bat as long as he could. Sluggo rolled one across the piece of tin.

"Can't hit a fly off the ground, Weenie. Here." Butch picked up the ball and threw it back, more at Sluggo than to him. Sluggo ducked and the ball rolled into Sandy's territory where it came to rest against a prickly pear. He nudged it away with his shoe, picked it up, pitched it back to Sluggo, then pulled out the cactus spines from the side of his worn-out sneakers. A passing pickup truck sprayed dirt and gravel on him.

The trio larked around for a half hour as the sun began to set.

"Okay, watch this. Like the Babe!" Butch pointed his bat at Sluggo, wiggled it around. "Right into Nona's kitchen." He pointed the bat in the general vicinity of Nona's parking lot, drew it back, flexed his wrists a few times, and Sluggo let fly. The pitch was waist high, a bit outside and slow, and Butch pounded it. The ball flew, headed south, climbed, banked at the edge of the parking lot, and began a gentle arc beyond Sandy who for the first time had to turn and run to chase down a fly ball, thus causing him to look *up* rather than *at* Highway 87, where Bart Sullivan steered Poppy's 1937 Ford Coupe toward the Magnolia Station. The car took the baseball full in the right front fender, one foot behind the headlights.

"Get out of the road! What a dumbass!" he shouted. Bart thought he had hit Sandy and screed the mechanical brakes to a sliding stop, then jumped out of the car. The boy, the ball, and the sun in Bart's eyes had come together to wreck his ambitious daydream of possible success with Carmen, last name forgotten, at the State Line. "What the hell do you think you're doing?" It didn't occur to him to ask if Sandy was okay, even after he saw the nose bleed. "Go home and fix your nose."

Sluggo and Butch ran up and seconded that Sandy's nose was bleeding. Butch looked for his baseball. Sandy again used his tee shirt to wipe the blood off his nose. Bart got back in the coupe and drove it toward the Magnolia Station. The boys followed.

When Homer walked out from the station hut Bart gunned the car to spin the tires on the gravel and braked hard to a stop at the pump, then rolled down the window.

"Two bucks." Homer put his hand on the window sill, a gesture that visibly irritated Bart. "And check the tires. You didn't check 'em last time." Bart sat back in the cushions and gazed off into the west, his thoughts of getting Carmen beyond first base punctuated by a relentless gong caused by the three boys, who were jumping up and down on the station's driveway air hose bell.

Homer wound up the crank on the gasoline pump until the gauge marked ten gallons, unscrewed the Ford's gas cap, put the nozzle in, and lifted the handle to start the flow. Bart watched him with a critical eye, fully expecting that for two dollars a man could count on more than having his tires checked and the windshield washed. *I shouldn't have to tell him to check the oil and water. If I'm putting in two bucks on Saturday night he ought to know I'm going on the road. Poppy wouldn't put up with that.*

While the pump gurgled gasoline into the Ford, the limping attendant bent down to unscrew a valve cap, pressed a tire gauge onto the valve, and noted that the sixteen-inch tire had less than thirty pounds of pressure. He stood up, walked around the coupe, untangled the air hose, and returned, gave the tire a few squirts of air, checked the pressure, and then screwed the valve cap back on. Bart drummed his fingers on the steering wheel while Homer put exactly thirty-two pounds in each tire.

"Forget something?" Bart could barely contain his irritation. "The water? The oil?" *I can't believe I have to tell the old bastard. Every time.* He shuddered to imagine if Homer had been so neglectful of the new Ford that Poppy hadn't bought.

There had been a 1942 four-door at the Ford house, sitting there for months after Pearl Harbor. Bart wanted Poppy to buy it but Poppy had said, again, that Bart needed to learn to "take the longer view." "People here are doing without. They like to believe we're sacrificing right along with them. And in a sense we are." Now, watching Homer check the battery, check the oil dipstick with a red rag, open the radiator cap, Bart thought that Homer should thank his lucky stars that Poppy hadn't bought that new Ford. If Poppy heard that Homer wasn't even taking care of the old car, well it would have been even worse for him if he had neglected a new one.

He handed two dollars to Homer who stood, waiting, until Bart peeled off the gas ration coupon and handed it over as well. He pushed the starter button, the engine caught, and Homer jumped back to keep Bart from spraying gravel on him in his rush to get on the Clovis Highway. Bart stepped hard on the gas pedal, shifted to second, spun the tires again to pick up speed, and never thought to look in the rear view mirror where he could have seen Homer shooting him the finger.

The baseball was scuffed where Bart's fender had knocked it back across the pavement. Sluggo squeezed it to see if it had been crushed. Butch tapped the bat against the concrete step of the station doorway. Sandy stood around watching Virginia's brother. They all looked up to watch Homer's farewell gesture, which produced a burst of laughter.

Homer limped back to the station, edged between the boys on the step, and went inside to put the two dollars in the cash register and sort the ration coupons into the drawer.

"What are you laughing at?" he snarled at them.

"Bart the Fart," Butch replied.

"What a turd," Sluggo chimed in.

Homer didn't reply, just busied himself between the oil can rack and a display of artificial additives guaranteed to extend every tankful and prolong motor life.

"Hey, Homer. How come he's always drivin' around? He don't have trouble buying gas. He even drives the three blocks from his house to the post office. Dad says we ain't supposed to be drivin' around like that because there ain't no gas to spare."

Homer ignored the question.

"Have you got any Super Bubble gum?" Sandy asked. It was generally superior to Fleers. He pushed three pennies over the glass counter. Homer counted out six pieces and gave them to Sandy. They were Fleers.

"Could I get Super Bubble instead? It's better'n Fleers."

"What's the difference? It's all sugar crap just the same."

"The wrapper." Super Bubble came wrapped in an offer to join the Superman of America Club. The waxed paper wrapping had comics.

Homer grumbled some more, replaced the gum, then slid the glass case door shut. Sandy handed over a piece to Butch and another to Sluggo, took one for himself, and pocketed the rest.

"Where'd you get the money?"

"I've been workin'."

"How come? School ain't out yet, not for a couple of weeks." Sluggo was in no hurry for summer. The end of school was the beginning of cotton hoeing season, a job worse than cleaning animal guts off the floor of his uncle's butcher shop.

Sandy didn't particularly want to tell them he was trying to save up for his father's birthday. They would razz him first for even talking about getting enough money to buy his father a car, then razz him again when he failed to do it. Instead he told them what he had done.

"Mr. Reilly lets me help stock groceries after school. I mow some yards. Old Bradley lets me sweep out. I might get Nona to let me wash dishes. On the weekends."

Sandy's industry was his friends' dismay. Butch, disdainful, figured it meant that Sandy's family was poor. Sluggo, envious, wished he had thought of Sandy's idea first, not because the jobs were inviting but because the worst of them was better than mucking out a slaughterhouse. Then Sandy said too much.

"Mostly I've been trying to help Mrs. Hastings. She's supposed to stay off her feet."

"Who's that?"

"Her husband's an Army captain. In the war. So I help around there, fixing up her wash house, cutting the grass, stringing up her clothes line. She didn't have a garden so I'm digging one up for her."

"Why can't she do it herself?"

"She's going to have a baby so she's supposed to have help. Doc said so."

"I know who she is. Miss Sullivan at the ration office. Don't know why they need *you* to do anything. She don't cook; they never eat at home. They go over to Nona's almost every night, just like it was home."

"That's 'cause they don't have a mother."

"Why not?"

No one knew.

"I know who you're talking about; his sister. Bart the Fart."

"Yeah. A pretty sorry fart, too." Sandy was emboldened by Homer having shot Bart the finger. "He never does anything around there, cut the yard or empty the trash barrel."

"My daddy says he's just a draft dodger. Poppy Sullivan got him the post office job so he wouldn't have to go to the army."

Homer listened to the boys but was smart enough to keep his mouth shut about Poppy Sullivan, and that meant to keep his mouth shut about the Sullivan kids, too. *Shouldn't have let them damned kids see me shoot Bart the bird*, he thought, *but he's just a prick*. Like everybody else, Homer knew that Poppy did a lot more than just run the newspaper. *Snap his fingers and see who jumps*. Everyone knew Poppy got Bart the job at the post office. They didn't know exactly how but, when the draft heated up, the old postmaster suddenly left town. Then Bart flunked his physical. Then someone named him postmaster. And when rationing came out — boom! Poppy's daughter was the ration clerk. The Sullivans always had plenty of ration cards; their friends figured out pretty quickly that if they wanted more gas or butter or even more plain hamburger than Franklin Delano Roosevelt thought they should have, well, it was a good idea to be one of Poppy's friends. It was a lot like the deal with the government men. No one knew how but Poppy always knew three or four days before when the government men were going to show up to buy everything. When they got to town, they always found the scrawniest cattle to buy, fewer bales of cotton, never an extra hanging beef or pig at the butcher shop or any extra butter in Reilly's cold locker. The government men never found a thing out of line, and every farmer, rancher, and shop keeper in Tierra took as good care of Poppy as he took of them.

"You boys shut your mouths. You don't know what you're talkin' about."

"I know this," Sluggo ran on, "Bart Sullivan's a queer." This was not true but Sluggo had a limited range of epithets for a draft dodger who had yelled at them for playing baseball when he happened to be wasting gasoline, and especially someone who could dress up on a Saturday night and drive over to Clovis without thought or worry about ration stamps or tires.

"And his sister's a hoor!" Butch was just repeating what he had heard Shirley say about Virginia. He was shocked, completely unprepared, when Sandy tackled him, flung him to the driveway, and was in the first stage of punching him in the face when Homer grabbed Sandy's fist in mid-air. Butch had crossed the line of what one could safely say about the Sullivans.

"You boys shut up. Get off him. What do you think you're doing?" He jerked Sandy off Butch who then tried to jump back up to hit Sandy. Homer grabbed Butch as well. For a grizzled old guy with a limp, Homer was a lot stronger than they had expected. "You boys just shut up. You don't know what you're talkin' about so stop it. You hear?" He shook Sandy and Butch by the shoulders. Sluggo stood a few feet away, gaping.

They said they heard.

"Ain't nobody worth fightin' about, not Bart and not his sister and not their folks neither. You boys don't know nothin' about them so stop shootin' your mouths off. Now, go on home, get out of here."

He finished off with a not-too-gentle shove in the direction of town. Sluggo fetched the bat and the baseball and they walked back across the vacant lot and toward the town square.

"Why'd you do that?" Butch demanded.

Sandy didn't answer him, in part because he wasn't sure what to say. Defending Virginia's honor seemed important, even though being her secret admirer got him little more than the right to shove a rusty old reel lawn mower over their sticker patch and clean out the neglected wash house. It wasn't like she had taken to him or spent a lot of time telling him stories about the war or, for that matter, even asking him to come by to do the chores he was doing. But he also remembered that Bart the Fart had made her cry when he had put her letters up on the post office wall, and she had picked him up off Reilly's floor to stop his nose bleed. Besides, he had heard Doc tell her to get some help, and Bart sure wasn't helping any. Defending her honor just seemed the right thing to do.

Bart had a different code of honor. He would have preferred the 1942 Ford, a model with the gear shift up on the steering column and a radio. *Floor shifts are obsolete. In fact, they're in the way. And I could listen to KCLO all the way.* KCLO played swing music for the army airmen who had been sent to Clovis. Bart liked swing.

Two miles west of Tierra, Bart drove past Cemetery Road. It was there, a mile off the highway, that he had maintained his social life in high school, the sale of Mason jar brandy having been his sole source of income and social contact. The former had come from the quarters and dimes forked over by the latter, his classmates who otherwise had little to do with him. The Cemetery Road was his business site because of the doubtful belief that it was too "spooky" for anyone to go after dark and therefore ideal for the sale of moonshine spirits. Bart formed a special sneer for the ghosts of Johnny Bradley and Hoyt Carter, then speeded up to forty-five miles an hour. *If I can hold it, I'll be at the State Line by nine-thirty and in Carmen's arms by nine-thirty-one.*

The setting sun was so bright that he had trouble seeing, its wide red reflection filling the entire horizon. As the bright color began to fade to dark red there was nothing that could block his progress. His plan was uncomplicated: find Carmen, get her drunk, get her into the coupe. To the list of the coupe's defects, no radio and a floor shift blocking access to Carmen's legs, he added the belief that the back seat of the 1942 model would be an advantage in fast-moving amours. He imagined Carmen in such a back seat, her thick black hair pushed up to the ceiling before falling back down around her shoulders. Her upper parts strained against the buttons of her clothes while her slender legs extended out from under a thin dress.

The last two times they had met she had rubbed her toes over Bart's ankle under the table. She had leered wide provocative grins at him, her dark eyes open and inviting, particularly to someone who had been alone with a female fewer than five times in his twenty-five years. She had taken his hand and drawn him away from the table, left the beers behind, and pulled him onto a saw dust dance floor peopled by aviators and their girls, *nothing like those bags in Tierra.* Bart wasn't much of a dancer but then, Carmen wasn't very demanding. *Just 'cause she's from New Mexico don't mean she's Mexican. Lot's of small women with dark hair and dark eyes. She's just the best one.* She had hinted rather frankly that the next time he might give her a lift, if he could afford it. He could. He was sure she would be waiting for him, and earnestly believed that the Ford people had built such a product precisely with this in mind. He accelerated to fifty, then saw some lights in the rear view mirror and eased the Ford back to forty-five.

A mile beyond Cemetery Road there were three or four real Mexicans, teenagers, Bart guessed, standing by the side of the road, hitchhiking from the labor camp. He didn't even slow down.

She'd better be waiting for me, that's all I've got to say.

Bart's threat was not precisely directed at Carmen. That he had missed her, and the State Line at Clovis, for much of the last month was not his fault. He couldn't prove what Virginia had done but, in Doc Pritchard's words, Bart had the worst case of gripes in the guts he had seen since the town had put in a clean water well. *Goddamn, Sullivan. You been eating out of a shit house? Wash your food, for God's sake.* She didn't admit to having done anything but Bart decided to settle the score by keeping every one of her letters. *I won't even put 'em up on the bulletin board,* he thought, as if posting Will's letters to her was a favor. He had the unformed belief that if people thought she was so damned special for getting knocked up, then he would let her tell them why Will Hastings wasn't writing any more.

And if I get to the State Line and Carmen ain't there, well, that's just one more thing I'll add to Virginia's bill. Damn her.

An hour later, Bart crossed into New Mexico. He downshifted to cross the railroad tracks, then angled across the highway and onto the dirt parking lot of the cinder block haven with the neon lights.

That there were only a dozen or so cars in the parking lot had not bothered him. That Carmen was not inside did. *Just eight-thirty this side of the state line. I'll wait.* He had a beer, listened to the juke box, and watched a few of the fly boys from Clovis Army Air Field hit on the local girls. Sitting alone, watching the soldiers, it occurred to him that he was the only guy not in uniform. That made him proud. His trousers, worn high with large pleats, were made of dark wool and contrasted with an open jacket and a casual shirt with an open collar. He considered himself natty. He had another beer, wanted to be conspicuous. A half hour later, he was still conspicuous.

"Hey, Ray. You seen Carmen?"

The bartender ignored him. Bart, under the illusion that Ray was his buddy, stood up and walked over to the bar.

"Ray! Hey! It's me. You seen Carmen?"

Ray looked up from washing glasses behind the wooden counter top. The cigarette smoke in the State Line formed a haze at eye level that competed with the odor of stale beer and Old Spice. A soldier pushed his way up to the bar, demanding two Black Labels. Ray pulled two bottles out of an ice chest, popped the caps off, and held them out to the aviator.

"Carmen? Who's Carmen?"

"Girl I'm always with. Cute, real small. Thick black hair. You know her."

Carmen had told him, when he gave her the ten dollars, that, "I'll put it to use the next time you're here." Bart accepted this as a commitment. Ray had been in the process of serving them two Blue Ribbons, and they clanked the bottle necks in accord. Ray had smiled and Bart had told him to keep the whole dollar. Ray should remember her.

Ray's tired look now suggested that, of all the girls who came in to hustle airmen and the few civvies still around, he had no idea who Carmen was. It was also plain that he couldn't place Bart, either.

"Oh, yeah, sure" he said, doubtfully. "Naw, not tonight."

"Was she in last night? Missed her."

Ray said he couldn't remember. Bart drank another Blue Ribbon, leaned against the rail and looked out on the dance floor. By his fourth beer he was sneering in the general direction of all soldiers in the room and privately alternating between the fury of being stood up and making the plans he would devise to punish Virginia for causing him to lose his grip on Carmen. He began to look around the dance floor and the tables for an alternate Carmen. *I'll show her; she doesn't want to show, there's plenty of girls waiting in line.*

However, none seemed to be waiting at the State Line, at least not for Bart. Not a single female sat by herself. Bart's efforts to cut in for a dance produced threats. He drank more beer. By midnight he concluded that Carmen was neither coming nor coming back, nor was anyone else lining up to get in the coupe's front seat and take her chances with the floor shift. He stiffed Ray the price of the last Blue Label, pocketed the quarters on his table, and left. As he started up the flathead engine, pulled on to Route 87, and turned east back toward Tierra, his anger escalated and his judgement declined with each shift of the obsolete transmission. Five miles later he made a decision.

Bitch, he thought. *Cheap little bar-hopping slut. Woulda been better to pick up one of them wetbacks.* He decided that Carmen needed to learn what it meant to stand up Bart Sullivan, and the Ford made a U-turn on the highway.

At fifteen minutes past midnight he had re-crossed the state line, which was open, and passed the State Line, which was not. He sped the remaining distance to Clovis, cruised along the dark highway and glanced up cross streets, then drove out of town as far as the Army air base. It was gated. He turned back. Re-entering Clovis, he peered at the few open gas stations and menudo huts, saw no one, and began to roam from one side street to the next.

I'll find the bitch, that's what I'll do. Tell her she can kiss my ass, that's what I'll do. Bart did not hold his liquor, even Blue Ribbon, very well. *Stand me up, I'll show her.*

A passing police car slowed when the officer noticed that the Ford coupe with Texas plates had trouble staying on its side of the road. "Home, this is Fourteen, out," the officer radioed. In a perfect world he would have turned around and stopped the coupe, but the world was no more perfect in New Mexico than anywhere else.

"Fourteen, you there?"

"Just said I was."

"You're supposed to say out."

"Out."

"Then go on over to the Paramount. You got a fight to break up. Out."

Fourteen reluctantly drove off in search of the fight rather than follow the Ford, a route that prevented the officer from seeing that Bart had begun to follow yet another car, an error made due to Bart's mistaken belief that the girl in the back seat was Carmen. Car Fourteen turned a corner and saw nothing of what followed.

"Hey, you!" Bart yelled at the airman in the front passenger seat. At the next stop sign he pulled alongside the car and rolled down the window. "Hey, you!" He yelled at the driver.

That airman rolled his own window down. He, and the other airmen in the car, and the two girls with them, saw a drunken civilian who, though it wasn't clear from his garbled speech, was saying, "No, not you. You!" and pointing a crooked finger at the back seat where the women were sitting. 'Where the hell were you?'

The airmen considered this to be rude. They were in the process of being trained to fly B-24 bombers. Part of their training involved the very practical matter of dealing with crash landings. Another part of the training involved the question of dealing with hostility on the ground after a crash landing. When Bart threw a second beer bottle through the open rear window of the airmen's Pontiac, the airman at the steering wheel reverted to his training. He rapidly let out the clutch and turned the front wheels hard so as to crash land into the Ford's grill. His passenger in the front seat, a twenty-three year old instructor of tail gunners, led an exodus from the sedan and assumed the stance he had used at Guadalcanal a year before, pausing only long enough for the other crew members to join him. When they did, the largest of them proceeded to remove Bart from the Ford coupe, using a technique known as "jerking the son of a bitch out of the car by his neck." It was at that moment that Bart got a good look at the girls in the back seat.

He remembered thinking, *Oh, not Carmen. Sorry.* Then Bart's personal headlights went out. Something that felt like a bowling ball hit his stomach and mouth a few times, then large strong hands shook him like a rag and dropped him on the pavement in front of the open door of Poppy's coupe. He heard the sound of car doors opening, then closing. The Pontiac drove away. Bart remained there for about fifteen minutes and was still slumped against the running board when the Clovis police officer came back, found him in a viscous puddle, and took him to the hospital.

"Open both eyes. Look at my fingers. How many fingers am I holding up?"

Bart wanted to vomit again. The collision between tail gunner's fist and Blue Ribbon stomach had not been gentle. The room spun around and Bart saw a man with a bright light strapped onto his forehead who was sticking a wooden tongue depressor into Bart's mouth and telling him to say, "Ahh," which only made Bart want to puke again. A blood pressure cuff on his arm began to inflate, hurting in its own special way. Just out of his range of vision he felt someone swabbing his face with alcohol; he flinched. The someone held up two fingers.

"I'm Dr. Martinez. Can you tell me where we are? Who's the president? What year is it?" Dr. Martinez was reasonably sure that Bart's only medical conditions were two black eyes, a very badly cut mouth, and a stomach that had been punched hard enough to prevent him from holding down the beer that had clouded his already poor judgement in the first place. Bart pulled his mouth away from the tongue depressor and said that they were in Clovis, that it was 1944, and that 'that "sonofabitch Roosevelt" was still president. Martinez was satisfied that cranial nerves two through twelve were intact and that Bart was oriented to time and place; the primary diagnosis was that Bart was stupid but no longer drunk.

"Nothing wrong with you that some BC Powder and a hot rag on your mouth won't take care of." Doctor Martinez filled out a patient form. "You feel clear-headed enough to drive?"

Bart said he did.

"He drunk, Doc?" the Clovis policeman asked. Bart's neck hurt when he swivelled around to see who was talking. For a brief moment he began to compose alibis.

"Not so I can tell. If he was, he isn't now." He handed the form to the policeman, who folded it and put it in his shirt pocket. "How old are you Mr. Sullivan?"

Bart told him.

"And what do you do?"

"I'm the postmaster in Tierra, Doc. *The* postmaster." Dr. Martinez jotted a few words on the patient form, then handed it to a nurse who tucked it into a clipboard.

"He's ready to go. The nurse will tell you," he turned to say to Bart, "what you need to do. Pay her your bill. Don't eat anything hard and no alcohol for a couple of days. Make that two weeks." Dr. Martinez walked out of the examining room.

Bart looked around and found his shirt and jacket on a hook on the door. On the other side of the door the Clovis policeman was standing, chatting with someone. When he saw Bart, he turned to speak.

"Saw your plates. Called a friend of mine to ask about the Ford coupe. You can thank your lucky stars, Boy, that I've got a friend in Texas."

Bart looked past the cop. Sheriff Hoskins was standing in the hallway, flipping his ten-gallon hat around in his hands, trying to get the nurse's eye. He heard Bart and the officer talking and turned to join them.

"I'll see he gets home," Hoskins said to the policeman. "Poppy's car's got some dents in the grille. Hope whoever ran into you didn't bust the radiator. Didn't see no water under it." He thought the car would make it back to Tierra and if not, he would follow Bart and take him on in.

Hoskins thought other men's sons weren't worth spit compared to their old men. Bart was no better than the run of the litter, worse than most. *Tell you what,* he told himself, *if that little shit hadn't been Poppy's boy I would have lined him up alongside Hoyt and Johnny and run him into the Army, too. But he* was Poppy's boy, so Hoskins' duty was to keep him out of trouble, no matter how stupid he was.

"Thanks for giving me a call." He and the Clovis policeman agreed that Hoskins owed him one.

The officer followed Hoskins to Bart's car, watched them start it up, then followed both of them out of town. He kept them in view until they drove past the state line into Texas, then turned back toward Clovis to finish the night shift, hopefully without another drunk on the streets.

Dr. Martinez at the hospital, lay down on a cot in the doctor's lounge. He closed his eyes and hoped to finish the night shift without another drunk in the emergency room.

Neither of them gave much thought to having cleaned up the one drunk who had gotten whipped pretty good. After the Army put the air field in town that was a common enough experience for both of them. But both of them would remember the one thing that puzzled them about the guy. "He wasn't in uniform — that's pretty unusual for a guy in good health." And then, "I wonder how that little prick dodged the draft?"

CHAPTER FIVE

June 1944

The romance was the talk of the ordinary people.

The imaginary elopement gave rise to endless conversations about Will Hastings ('such a good boy,' 'shame about his folks,' 'he'll be good for Virginia') and the ways of love and combat ('lot of them get married right before they go off to war'). Unaware that, after reading one of Virginia's letters to Will, Bart had elected to neither post any more of hers nor give any of Will's letters to Virginia, all who saw her asked how Will was holding up, where he was stationed, and what did he tell her about chasing Hitler back to Berlin. She lied to all of them.

Doc's intoxicated disclosure of her pregnancy satisfied everyone's suspicions but also fortified the town's brief love affair with Virginia and her growing bundle of joy. Praise for her elopement was superceded by a flow of feminine advice — what to eat, how much to walk, and what to do when the time came. Women stopped by the Sullivan home, and occasionally the ration desk at the courthouse, to leave nursery items old and new. Virginia accumulated bottles, nipples, rattles, infant clothes, and an array of dubious items completely foreign to her imagination and experience. Men winked when she went in to Nona's. Mrs. Claggert at the Dry Goods Store collected sewing patterns for baby clothes. Shirley's mother led a Baptist Ladies Bible Class Circle mission to teach Virginia how to cook, sew, and do laundry, skills Emma had not been able to impart before she was taken away. Like her father, Virginia once blamed Doc for not saving Emma from dementia. Unlike Poppy, Virginia had put the blame behind her in the struggle to grow up on her own. The Baptist Ladies were not a sufficient substitute, but they tried.

To her discomfort, Judge Oaks broadly hinted that when Virginia became too pregnant, he would have to let her go from the ration book office. "Lot of stairs here in the courthouse, Virginia. Don't want anything to happen." And Poppy continued to be smugly pleased that the town had rallied behind its first war bride and its first war baby.

Only Bart sulked at his sister's sudden popularity. The postmaster avoided baked goods, ate away from home, and sought a replacement for Carmen both at the State Line and, unfortunately, at points closer to home whenever he happened to notice girls from the Mexican labor camp walking along the highway of an evening.

"So, what about Captain Hastings? Is he okay? I mean, the war and everything?"

She didn't answer Sandy immediately, just continued to take Poppy's shirts out of the rinse tub and squeeze them through the wringer. Virginia had tolerated Sandy coming around to mow the lawn and help with chores precisely because he had not pestered her about Will or the baby, that and the fact that she did need some help. They had been doing laundry for an hour. In early June the wash shed was hot and smelled like Five Star bleach and grey water. There was only the one door and a window that didn't open. She took the hose and began to fill the last tub for rinse water. Her hair was dripping down her forehead and her clothes were wet. The baby had begun to kick, not painfully, but enough to let her know that whatever it was, it was being bounced around.

"Oh, he's not in any danger. Can you take this coil of hose and stretch it out there to the faucet?" Virginia pointed to a water hose that was rolled up and placed on the floor next to the door.

The water hose was new. Sandy figured that the Sullivans must have been lucky because his mother had sent him several times to buy a hose, only to be told that Franklin's hadn't been able to get any since 1942. He lugged the hose out the door and over to the faucet by the kitchen stoop, screwed in the fitting, and walked the other end back to the wash house.

They had finally cleaned out the bottom floor of the old well house and turned it into a laundry room. A tub with wringers was perched solidly above a concrete floor. Two tables were cleared off for Virginia to put dirty clothes on one side and clean ones on the other. A hole in the floor drained the overflow water outside onto a new vegetable garden.

"He's fine," she continued. "He's in England, not actually in the war." She had only a fuzzy idea of where the war in Europe was being waged, in part because the Army blacked out the names of towns in letters sent home and in part because most of the boys from the Texas plains were sent to the Navy and found themselves in the Pacific. It was the Japs who made Tierra mad. People considered that what happened at Pearl Harbor had happened to them personally and most boys were wading onto the beaches under the machine gun fire of treacherous little heathens hiding in caves and jungles. Moreover, there were a lot of old German names in town, dating from when the prairie was settled by Krugs and Meyers and even some Berliners. Many privately accepted that whatever it was the Germans were doing, they were doing it to Russians and Poles. They knew there was fighting in Italy but most people smiled and winked at stories of Italian guns that had never been fired and only dropped once. England was a long way from Italy. She finished wringing the shirts; they took a basket out to the clothes line.

"So, why's he in England? I know he's a doctor but is he going to be a soldier? Or a pilot? Why didn't he go to fight the Japs?" Sandy held up the tub full of wrung-out shirts while Virginia pegged them to the clothes line.

"Want something to drink?" she asked. Without waiting, she walked up the back steps and into the kitchen. A few minutes later she came back with two glasses and a letter. She sat down, patted the step beside her for him to come sit, and handed him a glass.

"Is it lemonade?"

"Not hardly. I haven't seen a lemon in years. Why'd you think that?"

"Ah, I just remembered the coconut and thought maybe you drank a lot of lemonade. What'd you do with the coconut? And the pecans?"

She smiled but didn't directly answer.

"It's apple juice. Sort of. I make it from whatever the birds don't eat," she said, pointing at a runty apple tree fighting for its life in the backyard. "You pick up the apples, cut them up and run them through a colander, then boil it a little."

It didn't taste very good. He wondered if it was something she liked because she was pregnant.

She handed him Will's letter.

"This is a V letter." She showed it to him, a single page folded to become its own envelope, with diagonal marks on the borders. It looked like the faded letters he had seen on the countertop at Bradley's barber shop. It was addressed to Virginia Sullivan, P.O. Box 7, Tierra, Texas, USA. "The Army copies soldiers' letters onto film and sends them over here, then puts them back on paper and mails them home to us. It says 'Captain Will Hastings, First Army FMO Trng Bn.' I'm not sure what that means. Then it says 'England.' except they blocked out where in England and then it says 'ETOUSA' and I'm not sure what that means either. Then it says 'care of the Army Postmaster NYC' and that means New York City. And this letter came all the way from England. Go on. Read it." She leaned back and took a sip of the apple water.

Sandy took the form and read it.

"'Dear Virginia: It's April now, finally not as cold here. I didn't know England was so cold. They've sent me to [~~marked out~~] for training. Finished TDY at Dr. Atkinson's clinic in [~~marked out~~].' The civilians don't have any — ' what's this word?'"

"Penicillin."

"Okay. 'Or Sulphur,' only he spelled it s-u-l-f-a, 'so I learned a lot about remedies, lots of ear aches, some ruptures, even helped deliver a baby. When I got back to Division the DMO said it was to get me ready for field hospitals, then he transferred me here to field surgeon school. Everybody's pretty decent except the major in charge. We used to get along but not any more. That's the army. Guess who else is here — that soldier I woke up and found handcuffed to me on the train from Scotland! No idea how he got away or wound up here, but his name's Douglas, he's a clerk and knows how to do everything, helps me out and no questions asked. He says he can find Peter over at 8th AAF and he'll hook us up with him in London when I finish school before we get shipped to [~~marked out~~].'"

"So, who's Peter? What's 8th AAF? Was he in jail?"

"No. No one was in jail. When Dr. Hastings first got to England he had to ride a train from Scotland to his army base. The army police handcuffed a soldier to him. They rode the train together, that's all. And Peter is his brother."

Sandy took this in. *Captain — Doctor Hastings had been handcuffed to someone on a train.* Visions of men in uniform flitted through his mind, then merged with other visions of a brother, an even more uncertain figure, who might be in the Army Air Force. As Virginia had feared, if Sandy started asking questions, and she started to answer them, a lot of things would begin to spill out.

"Why's he there? Is he from here? I don't remember anything about him."

"They're orphans. They lost their parents, a long time ago. I don't know much about it. When he was a boy the state sent him here to live and they sent his brother somewhere else." *And now they're back together,* she thought. *At least for now.*

"So is '8th AAF' the Eighth Army Air Force? Is he a pilot? What does he fly? Does he fly bombers? A lot of…" Sandy lost her in a torrent of questions about pilots and airplanes, the arcana of engines and propellers and speeds that boys knew but which women did not.

Virginia had not much been around boys. When they were girls, she and Shirley and Molly Cochran had made rag dolls with hair made from colored yarn and black thread eyelashes. They had coveted prohibited makeups and lipsticks and believed that becoming a cheerleader would improve their lives for as long as life mattered. The much-anticipated event of being alone with a boy in high school led to the discovery that boys were afraid of intimacy, yet cared deeply about motors and football. Bart, not having been among those boys, had been one of the creatures destined to be the last one chosen for a side, the obligatory valentine to whom every one in class must write a card.

Bart stayed out of the cotton fields and off the dock at the cotton gin by talking Poppy into letting him set news type at the *Times.* He was rather good at printing and great with the inks and solvents; by his senior year he had learned to distill peaches and apples and sugar to make mason jar brandy, which he sold in pints to anyone with a quarter. What Virginia knew about boys had not come from her brother.

"So, have you saved enough to buy a car?" she turned the questioning back on him before he got to any of the sensitive areas. "How much have you made?"

She also retrieved the letter. He hadn't turned the fold over to read the back side; he was so inquisitive that she didn't want to explain what Will had written there, not that she exactly understood it herself.

"Nine dollars." Sandy had made a little more than ten dollars since before Easter but some of it found its way into the box office at the motion picture show, some had been spent on bubble gum and a couple of Superman comics.

"When's your dad coming home for his birthday?"

"His birthday's tomorrow. The sixth. I guess he can't come today, with work and all, but he'll come home this weekend. For sure. Want me to bring him over? He's real tall."

"That'd be real nice, Sandy. Of course, if he hasn't been home for a while, he'll probably just want to see you and your mother."

"He makes Liberators. It's the biggest airplane in the war. It has four engines and carries more bombs farther than any airplane ever made. It's real good. That's what my dad does. In Fort Worth. Does Peter fly B-24's?"

Virginia may not have known much but she knew about B-24's. Like everyone else, she watched them fly in low over the town, open their bomb doors, and swoop along just above ground level on practice runs at cattle pens, buffalo lakes, water towers and windmills. They flew out of the Clovis army air field at all hours, popping up above Tierra without warning. They scared the wits out of her and most of the other women, but in a way that made them believe that America would not just win, but would hammer the Japs, and Hitler, too.

She also knew Sandy's father, though not well. He had worked at the cotton gin until the fire. She suspected that Poppy had helped him get the job in Fort Worth but that was just because Poppy had been on the phone for days after the fire, first to get the story out over the wire and, later, to badger insurance men, fire marshals, government buyers, anyone who had anything to do with the cotton gin or the bales that burned in it. A dozen men lost their jobs and went to work at Consolidated Vultee in Fort Worth. Just until the new gin is built.

She felt tired, more than she had expected. The temperature hovered near ninety but that had never bothered her before. She was trying to learn how to do things her mother had never quite taught her, and all at once. Since Emma had been taken away Poppy had just moved the family over to Nona's for dinner and to Mrs. Stuart's for laundry. The yard had been let go and no one had tried to raise a garden in three years. She wouldn't have taken these chores on now, either, if it hadn't been expected of her. "It's not just what people say, Virginia. They're always gonna say what they like, whether they believe it or not. It's what people do. And when your husband comes home he's not going to want to eat at cafés or have a yard full of stickers. He's going to want to see that baby up and walking, fat from food you cooked and toddling around in clothes you sewed. It's what women do, Virginia." She hated it, but Poppy was right.

He hummed around the house, making plans for Will to come home. "Will's going to take over Doc Pritchard's practice and we'll be rid of that quack." Poppy had picked out two or three frame houses for Will and Virginia and an extra lot just in case they wanted to build from scratch. He had quietly told the pharmacist to put Doc's clinic on a month-to-month rent because he "might be retiring after the war." "Fleming and I have an idea how to raise money for a new medical clinic, maybe even a real hospital, not just some place for people to go have babies or get their legs set and die." Poppy's whirlwind took no notice of Virginia and, two months after she found out that she had eloped, she also found herself doing laundry and cremating rationed roasts and potatoes. She was like any other bride, except for the technicality of a husband.

"Sandy, I need to rest, so run on home. Thank you for coming over to help." She struggled up to her feet, then stood and arched her back to relieve some of the stiffness of the extra pounds she carried. It was four in the afternoon and, for some reason, she was not only tired but also she had a sense of unease, as if something bad was happening to her. "Everything else can wait."

Sandy hemmed and hawed a few moments and it occurred to her that he might be standing by to see if she would pay him for helping with the laundry. Since she had last paid him for anything he had mowed her lawn, such as it was, picked the early tomatoes from the garden and weeded the rows, hauled off loads of junk from the washhouse, and put the chicken wire back up on the fence posts to keep the neighbor's chickens out of the vegetables.

"If it's okay I'll just keep it on a list and pay you Saturday — no, Friday! — so that you can add it to your savings for your Dad's birthday." She felt so tired that she didn't even want to go in and rummage around looking for change or, for that matter, the job list she had kept for Sandy.

"It's okay. I need to be at Mr. Reilly's in a few minutes, and I've got to clean the barber shop too. It's Monday."

She watched Sandy leave across the backyard, skirt around the struggling apple tree, and walk in the direction of town. Virginia opened the screen door and entered the kitchen, then trudged as far as the table before deciding that she had to pull out a chair.

This isn't like me, she thought.

She had been uneasy for several days, as if something was happening just beyond her reach. Now she found herself almost paralyzed, and without explanation. *I can barely move. I have got to sit a minute and then get to bed. Dinner will have to wait.* The thought of cooking troubled her, not because of the smells or lifting or chopping, but because it involved lighting a fire on the stove. Something about the image of a steel skillet descending into flames, the sizzle of burning hamburger, frightened her and would not leave.

She caught her breath, then struggled to her feet and down the hall to her bedroom. She sat, kicked off her shoes, and deliberately lay back, head on pillow, carefully lifting her legs together to settle them on the covers. The afternoon light struck the mirror on her bureau and she considered pulling the shade down but, for no reason she could articulate, the idea of being in the dark made her afraid. She closed her eyes and waited, trying to ignore the uneasiness.

Two hours later she jerked awake from a nightmare, shouting his name. Even after she opened her eyes she sensed that she was trapped inside of something. It was dark and cold and loud like rushing wind, and she couldn't see out. She was strapped in and no matter what she did she couldn't get free. The thing began to fall, the straps restraining her, and suddenly there was a hellish explosion of thunder and flashes, a crash as the thing slammed into the earth and broke apart. The last image she saw was a night sky full of fire, and then total and complete darkness, silence, and — nothing.

Nothing of the kind had ever happened to her, not when she learned she was pregnant, nor when her mother had been taken to the hospital, nor even when he had got on the bus for the last time, bound for shipment to England. She felt hot tears and the sweat that had soaked her hair and the pillow and covered herself, trembling, certain that somewhere something was going very badly. It was five in the afternoon of June the fifth, in Tierra.

Poppy Sullivan sat at his desk in the two rooms that made up the office of the *Tierra Times*. Thursday's edition was already composed, stories about predicted cotton prices and the number of head of baby beef that the OPA buyers had contracted. He had wrapped the local advertisements around a bomber attack on Romanian oil fields. The courthouse schedule was posted adjacent to news of a two percent Series E War Bond. Bounding Home had won the Belmont. It was the usual pile of lines he put in the paper, things no one read. Everyone got the war news off the radio and, as for local details, things that needed knowing were passed between the men who needed to know them, one way or the other. That is how he learned about the men in the dark green sedan.

"Poppy, you free?" the voice had come over the telephone. Hoskins hadn't said his name, nor did he have to. Within ten minutes the sheriff had slipped in the back door of the *Times*.

"Listen. I looked out my window at the jail and there was that green sedan." He paused to let Poppy grasp the story. "It parked there at the curb and two of them got out and, listen to this, they went into the bank."

Poppy sat back in the wooden chair and crossed his fingers but said nothing. Hoskins could tell from Poppy's knitted eyebrows that this was a concern.

"They was there maybe an hour. I watched 'em drive off. Homer called and said they went back east." Back east was toward Lubbock. There was no doubt they were government men.

Poppy asked a few details, any special markings on the car, how the men were dressed. Hoskins had no particular facts. He thanked the sheriff who said, "Just thought you'd want to know," and, by his nod, indicated that the service was appreciated. Hoskins left.

Green sedans had come and gone often enough. OPA auditors arrived at the courthouse once a month to check Virginia's work at the ration desk. They picked up expired coupons, delivered new ones together with cards and ration books, and checked her bookkeeping to see that the registers matched the family names and numbers of people in the households. They found a mistake here and there, exactly the same errors found in little towns all over the Lubbock area, but not once did they spot anything to make them suspicious. Virginia had been the perfect choice, a girl smart enough to do the job, honest enough to do it right, and young enough to make a few ordinary mistakes.

There had been other government men, too. They came to the co-op to collect the warehouse receipts and to check the numbers against the records at the cotton compress. Some went to the county agent to check cattle records and keep track of the herds for contracts. A few stopped in now and then at the meat market and over at Reilly's Grocery, trying to pass themselves off as just ordinary travelers who dropped in to buy something to eat in the car. Men in government cars were common enough in Tierra and everywhere else. None had ever gone to the bank before.

Poppy wondered whether Fleming had the stomach to talk with them. Fleming had been a weak link but one that he couldn't do without. It was possible, in fact probable, that the government men were just ordinary bank examiners, come to look at the loans on the books. Poppy had told Fleming and every other banker in the area that all of Roosevelt's new rules meant that there would be government men like they had never dreamed of coming in to look at their books. Poppy had joined in their universal complaint that Roosevelt's government was a bunch of socialists; privately he thought it was a good idea to have someone smarter than Fleming take a look at the books now and then. Even if he couldn't say it in public, the closing of banks and the lynching of mortgage agents in the Depression had been pretty good signs that something needed fixing.

He considered the problem from all angles. If the government men wanted to compare cotton receipts to crop loans, Fleming had the records and they could look. There wasn't a chance in a million that they would find a record that would get anyone excited. If they wanted some other record, Fleming didn't have any other records. They had discussed this before, back when the crop loans had been paid off. It was not a subject for the *Times* and not a subject Fleming would want to discuss. Poppy had been over it in his mind a hundred times. The men in the green sedan could come and go all they liked.

At six o'clock Poppy decided that he would do nothing. He could finish the next edition in a couple of hours on Tuesday, make a few calls Wednesday afternoon, and let the summer take its course one week at a time. The cotton fields were so thin that they made the weeds look good. Cattle pens were listless, the scrawny feeder calves wandered from pasture to pen and back in search of anything to eat while the barns were closed tight and the better head of livestock well out of the way of county agents and curious government buyers.

At six-fifteen he noticed that the light had become dim. An hour before the sun coming through the street door window had been so bright that he had lowered the shade; now it was all but dark inside. Poppy walked to the door, opened it, and saw that while he had been pondering green sedans and bankers, a huge, dense, and very black cloud had filled the sky. He stood there, watching, scratching his chin, nodding hello to the men at the abstract office and the women next door at the dry cleaners. When he turned his gaze toward the courthouse the first drop of rain hit him square in the forehead.

It doesn't rain in June, Poppy thought. It was as odd as finding a bowl of sugar on the table or discovering that Bart had left a full tank of gasoline in the Ford — possible, but not likely. The second drop, and third, fourth, and all the rest were huge, pieces of water so large that they splattered on his head and brought the smell of dirt with them. The constant prairie wind had backed down as well, and the dust that hovered over the town was being settled back onto Tierra by a freak rainstorm. He wondered if Bart had thought to roll up the car windows.

He also wondered whether Virginia had tried again to make supper. The fact was that Poppy hated her cooking. Emma had been a biscuits and gravy kind of woman, a girl who could fry up a chicken. He knew it wasn't fair to dislike Virginia for not being Emma but there wasn't anything he could do to stop it. Poppy couldn't think of anything in particular that Virginia had done that was so bad, not even getting pregnant, but whatever he blamed Virginia for, and mostly he blamed Virginia for not being Emma, Poppy wanted to forgive it all because she had gotten Will Hastings. When Will came home Poppy would personally drag Doc Pritchard by the neck, take him to the city limits, and throw him out of Tierra in a New York minute.

The crack of lightning changed the *Times* from dark to bright, then dark again, and not three seconds later the boom of thunder told him that the storm was close by. He grinned at the thought that just maybe the freak storm would flood out the government men driving back to Lubbock in their green sedan. Another thunderclap prompted him to consider that it might help Fleming remember that silence is golden. He couldn't decide whether to sprint across the street to the post office to catch a ride home with Bart, to wait out the storm and walk home, or to just set out on foot and get soaked, when another sound came through the small news room.

• •

///// 6june44//// OWI-1 FLASH BULLETIN ////
SUPREME HEADQUARTERS ////
1:09 Universal War Time ///
Stand by for bulletin next hour
ETOUSA HQ London////

• •

It was the news wire printer. Poppy waited for the clack of the printer to finish, then took the paper, held it to the light, and read the cryptic note.

Bah, he thought. *Stand by, my butt.* It wasn't the first time he had been told to wait for a war bulletin that never came, not from Supreme Headquarters London. The war news all came from the Pacific. *Navy does a hell of a lot better than all those idiots in London.* He decided to make a run for home, only three blocks away. He looked out the window a last time, saw the rain coming down in sheets, and found a cardboard box to carry over his head for an umbrella.

Poppy stepped out the back door, held the box up, locked the door, then trotted down the alley in a jog that only made his ankles sink into the mud. He turned the corner by Franklin's Lumber Yard, faced east away from the driving rain, and decided he was too far in to turn back. It was only as he neared the house that it occurred to him:

Did they ask Fleming where the cotton gin men were working now? He decided he would have to find out and, if need be, make a few calls to Fort Worth.

By the time he got home, Poppy was indifferent to the rain and frankly relieved that Virginia had not begun to cook. She said she wasn't feeling too well, and he said that they would wait for Bart to drive home in the coupe, then go up to Nona's on the highway for a decent meal. As bad as the idea of food sounded to her, being alone sounded worse.

They waited until almost nine o'clock before Bart drove home in the coupe. He said only that he and Doc had been talking and he didn't feel like dinner. At Nona's, Poppy asked for a pork chop and mashed potatoes. Virginia said she wasn't hungry. Nona wanted to close and had no idea why God had dumped the Sullivans on her at nine o'clock on a rainy night, but she brought them both a hamburger patty, a bowl of tomato soup and some toast. "That's all that's left in the kitchen," she said to them. They accepted it.

They finished the begrudged hamburger patties and Poppy drove Virginia home, then went back to the *Times* to use the telephone there to call a friend in Fort Worth. One advantage of owning the newspaper was not having to share a party telephone line. A disadvantage was that a newspaper often received news and, late at night on June 5, 1944, already the next day in France, the *Times* received the news. When Poppy unlocked the back door he heard the news wire go off again.

Should've shut the damned thing off, he said to himself, then pulled the teletype sheet out of the printer and read that the invasion of Europe had just begun across the English Channel.

///// 6june44/// OWI-2 FLASH BULLETIN ////
SUPREME HEADQUARTERS ANNOUNCES
ALLIES BEGIN OPERATIONS ON NORTHERN
COAST OF FRANCE //// WASHINGTON

Poppy read it, then read it again. This was the bulletin that he had been told several hours earlier to stand by for. He looked at his watch; it was after ten in the evening. He wondered what time it was in Europe.

No matter how long Poppy stared at the wire printer, it just stared back. He thought to pick up the telephone, call Fort Worth, and go home. But if the bulletin was correct, if that wishy-washy Eisenhower had finally put his pants on, this might be the real invasion. *But it just might be a goddamned fishing boat somebody blew up in the English Channel or another raid on some gambling town like those idiots tried a couple of years earlier.* He was skeptical. But if this was the real thing, the "assault on fortress Europe," it could be a very good thing.

Poppy thought of the possibilities. He could put out a special edition. For free. He could call in every advertiser he had ever had plus a few more who had never spent a dime at the paper, and tell them he needed a little help to make up the cost of the Wednesday special. He thought of how to phrase it: *Ed — Poppy down here at the paper. Listen here. I'm doing up a patriotic edition for Sunday, something real special for the boys. So I'm calling you and all the men who support the troops to make sure you want to show a little support on Sunday. That's right, for our boys. Yep. Oh, it'll cost a little more than usual, because of the colors and all...* Most wouldn't ask the price; those who would, mostly German families anyway, *it's in their blood, careful with a dollar,* he would tell them and they would yelp and he would say that they didn't have to advertise, it was just for people who wanted to support the troops. If he handled it right he could make as much out of Sunday's edition as he would normally make in six months. And if the invasion succeeded, well, he could do it again, every time the troops moved. He wondered why the Navy hadn't handled the war news that way; he could have been making money ever since the Battle of Midway.

He compromised by turning on the radio. At nearly midnight the Philco popped and crackled, an urgent voice broken by static on the air:

.... We interrupt this program to bring a special bulletin from London. A report from German TransOceanic News states that allied forces have begun the invasion of Europe, landing on the beaches of Northern France. There has been no confirmation from the combined Allied Command....

Poppy waited for more news, waited to see if it was a false alarm. The Germans had announced the invasion before, whether to get Eisenhower to tip his hand or out of jitters no one knew. However, a few minutes later, the static returned.

.... Again, there has been no confirmation from combined Allied Command. However, the BBC reports that all persons within eighteen miles of the English Channel are to stay off the roads and stay away from docks and railway lines. Dutch radio reports that....

That was enough for Poppy. He waited.

• •

///// OWI-3 FLASH BULLETIN //// SUPREME HEADQUARTERS ANNOUNCES A COMMUNIQUE FROM SHAEF: "UNDER THE COMMAND OF GENERAL EISENHOWER ALLIED NAVAL FORCES, SUPPORTED BY STRONG AIR FORCES, BEGAN LANDING ALLIED ARMIES ON THE NORTHERN COAST OF FRANCE. BOMBARDMENT OF GERMAN INSTALLATIONS BY THE BATTLESHIPS TEXAS AND ARKANSAS AND UNITS OF ALL

ALLIED FORCES PRECEDED LANDINGS BY
INFANTRY TROOPS NEAR CHERBOURG FRANCE"
////3:34AM WASHINGTON

As the night wore on, Poppy composed the wire stories into a single sheet edition. He had neither the skill nor the manpower to plagiarize the *New York Times*. There were no photographs, no maps, and only the barest of stories about airplanes and paratroop landings. But by six in the morning, Poppy had printed a special edition with the huge headline:

ALLIED ARMIES INVADE NORTH OF FRANCE

He took twenty copies to Nona's, where she was making the first coffee for the farmers who came in the mornings. He took another fifteen over to the cotton co-op and put them under a brick next to the front door. He dropped off a dozen at the front door of the drug store, another dozen at Reilly's Grocery, six at the courthouse, and a few at the gas station. Poppy had gone to the post office before anyone got their mail, stuffed a folded sheet into every mail box, and tacked two onto the bulletin board next to the war bond posters and the draft board notice. He took one copy to the telephone exchange. Poppy may have gotten the geography wrong — it should have said, "In Northern France" instead of "North of France" — but by seven-fifteen in the morning, almost every person in Tierra and every farmer in the county knew what had happened.

On Sunday Reverend Crates, drawing his lesson from King David, preached a sermon of war. "Tierra, like every town, is on its knees to God in prayer for our boys overseas. We pray for them to come home safe, Lord, to come home to mothers and sisters and farms and fields, Lord. And to come home victorious!"

"Hallelujah!"

"Amen!"

"I hear people say Thou Shalt Not Kill! That this war is wrong. That I do not believe God will look with favor on a nation that kills. It's true." It was not true; no one had criticized the invasion of France in any way, but Reverend Crates thought it powerful to demonize mythological doubters. "But I tell them, 'Brother, the Lord is a just God, and a fair God, but he is not a God who says there will be no war.' He tells us in the Psalms that King David knew about war. There will be sadness and grieving before there is victory. Even David the warrior knew grief. We learn from the Book of Samuel that..."

Reverend Crates preached the sermon of David and Bathsheba. A more carefully educated minister of the gospel might not have confused King David's war to kill both Uriah at the city gates and also the child born to his king and his wife in his absence.

> "... David said to his servants, 'Is the child dead?' They said, 'He is dead.' Then David arose from the earth, and washed, and anointed himself, and changed his clothes; and he went into the house of the LORD, and worshiped."

Reverend Crates intended his words as advance comfort to the flock, completely unaware of what some sheep heard. Shirley heard Reverend Crates use parables to say that Virginia was a harlot, like Bathsheba. Virginia, already reeling from one forewarning, feared he was preaching a pointed admonition for her own pregnancy, one she privately acknowledged was not especially cleansed by Poppy's dubious wedding announcement. Poppy and most parishioners heard what they wanted to hear as well, and concluded that God was on their side.

Sandy heard none of it, and went home sad.

"Sorry about your dad," Sluggo had said.

"Ah, it's all right. They need him in Fort Worth. What with the invasion and all." Sandy said it because his mother had said it, but she hadn't sounded like she believed it, not when his father had called to say he couldn't come home. Sandy didn't sound like he believed it either.

Poppy and Virginia were celebrated after the service. Most of the congregation stood in line to shake Poppy's hand. "Good paper today, Poppy," they had told him. "Real patriotic, and about time." "Something good in the news," they had said, proud of the wire stories of battle glory moving up off the Normandy beaches, ignorant of the thousands of boys killed or shot up and bleeding just a mile or two inland.

Nona and Mrs. Tarlton used one corner of the vestibule to trade observations of Virginia at dinner Monday evening:

"Well, Poppy seemed agitated. And Virginia? Well, I never saw anybody so jumpy. It's not like she puked or anything, not sick like that. It was like, oh, I don't know, she was staring off out the window, and real upset."

"Like Emma used to get," Mrs. Tarlton added, to remind them that Mrs. Sullivan had been not only a saint but otherworldly as well.

"No, not like Emma," Nona continued. "It wasn't like that. Virginia was all jumpy, but there wasn't anybody there. Besides, the lightning and thunder was over. Course it was raining still."

"It's because she knew poor Will was in danger, even before it came on the radio."

"Or in the papers."

"That's right."

Thus Virginia was briefly renowned for having been visited by a spirit of some kind, a premonition of the invasion, with psychic knowledge that the man she loved was in harm's way.

It was the Sullivans' finest hour.

CHAPTER SIX

July 4

"I'm going over to Clovis. You'd like it — hop in."

She said no, but got in the car anyway.

"How old are you?"

She might be sixteen but he figured she would pass for eighteen.

She lied, and said nineteen.

CHAPTER SEVEN

July 1944

Because of the rain Nona's was busier than usual. There was only so much that the farmers could do with muddy fields, flooded barns, overflowing pig pens and stables. The men at the co-op were idled just as effectively. Most found an excuse to come into town and, once in town, stopped by to see if anyone had any news. They stayed for a cup of coffee, maybe a bite, and Nona found herself hopping until after lunch. It wasn't until after the last of them got up from the table and moseyed back outside that Poppy told Sheriff Hoskins he thought he had been drinking. Hoskins denied it.

"Jesus, Hoskins, there's red mud all over the squad pickup." The squad pickup was the Dodge truck which Tierra County bought for the sheriff's office. "Where are you going to get red mud on the damned thing if you haven't been out to the dobes?

"So what if I was out there? Don't mean I was havin' a drink, does it? I got my responsibilities." Hoskins resented Poppy's control. It was an old resentment, one common between lifelong friends, one smarter than the other. Hoskins made a show of self-sufficiency by wearing his star on a white shirt and tried, with his ten gallon hat and roping boots, to give the impression that he was a working cowboy named sheriff by a grateful town. He believed with all his small mind that no one knew he stopped by the *Times* several times a day, always through the back door. He was stung when word once got back to him that Mrs. Tarlton had told the women at the beauty shop that Hoskins had grown a mustache so Poppy's butt wouldn't itch so much. The fact is that Hoskins would later testify that he never did anything unless Poppy told him to do it.

"I get calls on them wetbacks, got to go see what they're gettin' into. We need them damned fields to dry out, get 'em back to work." Hoskins feigned weariness and dismay from the rigors of controlling a throng of hot-blooded Latinos from knifing, fornicating, and drinking their way into his empty jail.

It had rained off and on for over a month. The cotton fields were bursting, stalks thick and tall from the rain, fuller and more dense than anyone had ever seen in the scant decades of cotton farming in that part of West Texas. When the rains did recede the fields got just dry enough for the Mexicans to get in to weed and clean the rows. No sooner would they get the crops in order than the rains returned. Even the cattle ranchers were beginning to tire of it, their pastures so green that the cattle were fattening up before they could hide all the good ones from the government buyers. That was not a problem that the cotton farmers had; the first picking was months away and in the twisted market logic of cotton futures, a great crop could mean low prices come November. To make it worse, the Mexican workers threatened to move on if they didn't make any pay while they sat in their adobe huts five miles out of town. In Hoskins' view it was better to let them do their drinking out at the labor camp than to have them coming into town. Besides, it was a dry county, and the men had to get a bottle somewhere.

"So, what'd you do? Bust up somebody's tequila still?" Poppy snorted at Hoskins' claim to have been on a law enforcement mission. He only went out to the camp to get a drink or to pester the senoritas. He wondered whether somebody would stick a knife into Hoskins one day. "Why don't you just leave 'em alone? Long as they're out there, they ain't hurtin' no one. If you run 'em off, the farmers — well, they vote for sheriff too, you know."

Hoskins sulked at the rebuke. He did have a drink at the labor camp, but just one, and that just to show the wetbacks that he wasn't going to work them over for making a false report. The fact was that he had been out there on a law enforcement mission, but not one he could tell Poppy about. Somebody had given one of the girls a lift to Clovis for a little July Fourth celebration of his own making and got her drunk. When she finally made it back home she was a little roughed up. Hoskins suffered in silence, agitated by a common belief between lifelong friends, that the other man's son isn't worth half as much as his old man. Hoskins would do whatever he had to do to make sure Poppy's sorry son hadn't gotten into any real trouble; that was part of being Poppy's friend.

The door opened, a crack of hot sunlight came through, Arnie appeared. The slight little man peered around to adjust his eyes to Nona's darker dining room, settled on Poppy, and swished over to the table.

"Sit down, Arnie. You got a tic?"

Arnie's eyes darted to see if anyone else was in ear shot. He sat almost all the way down to the chair, stood back up, peered again, ran a finger round the inside of his collar, then sat again.

"Listen, Poppy. D'you hear the train? It just pulled out. Tried to call you."

"So, Arnie, whatcha got?" He waited. Arnie waited even longer.

"Listen, Poppy, I thought maybe you might want to come over to the depot with me. If you've got a minute."

Arnie's voice had a note, a bit of a squeak but something else, a hesitation, a hoarse whisper, even. *Something's got him nervous*, Poppy thought. *Something he don't know what to do about.*

"Sure, Arnie. Is something wrong?"

"No. I don't know." Arnie was so agitated he could barely stay in the chair. "I need to know what to do. With something."

Hoskins listened intently, acting as if he were included in the conversation.

"With something?" Hoskins chimed in. "You need the truck?"

Poppy glanced at Arnie, who shrugged his shoulders to indicate that it was a bigger problem than he knew how to answer.

"Let's take the truck. Hey, Nona! I'll be back. Hang on to my cup." Hoskins never actually paid Nona for the coffee he drank, a fact she tolerated because most of his coffee came with Poppy sitting across the table from him. She was not one of the needy citizens who had sought out Hoskins for office, but at least he didn't cost her much.

Arnie shuffled out the door and walked back across the highway to the depot. Poppy and Hoskins climbed in to the cab of the muddy truck and backed away from Nona's parking lot, then chugged across the road in the direction of the railroad tracks. Prairie dogs popped up from burrow holes to watch the truck edge along the dirt street.

Poppy considered whether to mention the phone calls to the sheriff. People had called to thank him for ration coupons he had not gotten for them. Mrs. Tarlton, of course, stopped by Thursdays and Mondays to tell him what she had liked in the newspaper after she had fished hers and Bradley's out of her mail box. She irritated him such that when she talked about red stamps and wheat-colored stamps and getting a half pound of sugar in Lubbock, he heard only half what she had said. But Mrs. Reilly had told him it was nice what he had done for July Fourth, all that brisket and whatnot. Franklin at the hardware appreciated how he had come up with enough blues and a spare booklet so they could get a couple of kegs of nails, well, they hadn't actually used the ration books for nails, they had passed them on to the Keuhlers for something and the Keuhlers had gotten a government contract for more hogs so they got a permit to build more sheds and they let Franklin parley that into extra nails and plywood, which he had put to use. He had gotten Franklin some water hoses, not a hard thing to do, but he knew nothing about the nails or the briskets or Mrs.

Tarlton's sugar or anything else. It seemed to Poppy that a lot of people had experienced some good fortune the last month or so. He didn't mention it to Hoskins.

They drove past the cotton gin, now out of use until picking season. Beyond it there was the compress and the burned warehouse, what was left of it. Seven months after the fire it still looked harsh in the sun. Dust and charred bits of tin and wood that had been rafters, door frames, warped siding, all flapped in the dusty air. The burned shell of the west end remained more or less as it had been after the volunteers had put the fire out. Empty cotton trailers, left in the same clutter as before the fire, added to the air of abandonment. Neither man said a word.

After the fire Poppy had published a story in the *Times*, then sent it out over the wire.

• •

/// Tierra: Texas News Service: /// Area cotton bales ravaged in fire...///

• •

Over the next few months Poppy heard from people in Lubbock, Brownfield, even as far as Angelo, that they had read about the fire. "What a shame," they said. "Must 'a really hurt the farmers." He had assured them that it had hurt the farmers. The compress had been saved but the bales of cotton in the warehouse with the gin were not. There had been a consensus in the community to not talk about it any more and now they didn't even look at the place.

Fifty yards on they caught up with Arnie standing on the platform of the Santa Fe depot. Arnie watched the pickup grind to a halt, Hoskins grinning at skidding the tires to create a cloud of dust that settled on the slight little man. Poppy silently wished that Hoskins wasn't always a prick, but he was, and there hadn't been much to choose from. The sheriff was what the sheriff was. The men got out of the truck and walked up the cement steps to the platform, shook hands with Arnie as if they hadn't seen him five minutes earlier, and followed him in silence across the platform to the diminutive ticket office-waiting room-telegraph office-freight storage. When they were all inside Arnie peered out the windows to the tracks, then to the dusty road and, satisfied no one was within a hundred yards of the place, motioned Poppy to follow him around the counter.

"Okay, Arnie. Show me what's up. You seen a ghost?"

Arnie pointed to a plywood box on the floor.

The box, painted a dull green, was bound with hinges on the top. The corners had been reinforced with wood bracing. Opposite the hinges someone had sealed the box with two pieces of metal bent in a right angle and screwed heavily into the wood and braces. It looked like a smallish version of a cheap, square, plywood coffin.

"Look here, Poppy." Arnie stepped around the box, taking care to not touch it. Poppy followed him and, without invitation, Hoskins crowded in to get a look as well. "See this here? This here's the bill of lading." He looked up to see if Poppy was following him. "The shipping document." The bill of lading was a government form, a single page of printed blocks and small typeset, taped firmly beneath a clear plastic sheet to protect it from the weather. Poppy bent down over it and squinted. Someone had written in a very heavy hand the lading instructions.

> Eighth Army Command, High Wycombe,
> Bucks, England, ETOUSA
>
> To: Captain Woodrow Wilson Hastings
>   care of Miss Virginia Sullivan
>   General Delivery, Tierra Texas
> via: first available

The men studied the box, the bill of lading, then the box again. Arnie held his breath.

"I called you as soon as the train left, Poppy. I saw this and I thought Jeez, what am I gonna do about this? And I called you. Then I figured you must be over at Nona's, so…"

"Thank you, Arnie. Thank you very much." Poppy paused, stared at the label, then stood up.

"What do you think it is, Poppy? Do you think it's…?" Arnie couldn't carry on. They could see he was visibly upset.

"Is it what, Arnie?"

"His…you know. His…remains?"

"Remains?"

"Yeah, his remains. Little Will's? You know…"

It dawned on Poppy what had upset Arnie to such a degree. He thought Will Hastings had been killed in action, that his body had shown up on Arnie's train platform like so much grain or cotton and it was his burden to tell.

"You mean like his body? No, Arnie, not at all. Will? Is that what you're worried about? Naw, I'd know because of the news wires. You haven't seen anything come through on the telegraph, have you?"

Arnie agreed that he hadn't.

"Besides, I don't think they'd send him home in a box." Poppy smiled gently and put his hand on Arnie's shoulder, a gesture he had learned from his father.

Arnie took it as a sign of reassurance but he was still trembling, his shirt soaked with sweat. Yet, Poppy's assurance that young Hastings had not been dumped into a wooden crate for shipment home was not confirmed and, in any event, if the box didn't contain Will's corpse, what did it contain?

"Ain't no body in there, Arnie," Hoskins echoed. "Seen a guy over in Lubbock. At the glider school. Ast him about it 'cause of the Bradley boy, him an' the Carter kid. Course, ain't the same, them over in the Philippines and all, but same Army. Anyways, he says naw, Army ain't sending bodies home, just buries 'em right there. Kid gets shot and Army rounds 'em up, throws 'em all in a pile with the others got shot that day, makes the niggers take 'em to the rear and dig graves right then. Course they get the dog tags and all to be sure who they is, but they ain't sending nobody back home. So don't worry about no corpse here in the depot. Specially not little Hastings."

Hoskins' wisdom was both reassuring and depressing. The satisfaction that the army would not send Will's body home in a crate came with the reminder that Hoyt Carter and Johnny Bradley had not been heard from since the Japs overran MacArthur at Bataan. Arnie had been the man to bring the telegram out to the Carter farm. That had been more than two years ago.

"Besides, I'd have gotten it off the wire, Arnie," Poppy added. "War Information sends that out every day. I know the name of every boy killed or wounded from all over West Texas. Anyhow, Will ain't in danger of gettin' shot, not in the medical corps. He's all right. But even if some bomb or something hit him, I'd have gotten it off the wire service."

The men gazed at the box a few moments more before the next question popped out of Arnie's mouth.

"Why'd the army over in England be sending something to Will here? I mean, it says 'To Captain Woodrow Wilson Hastings.' To him, not from him. That's what it says. But he's in the army there. Seems like they'd know that and send it to him there. Or just hand it to him. England ain't such a big place. Don't make sense."

Poppy knew or, as he said to himself, he was "97% certain" why the Army was sending something to Will. He studied the bill of lading and concluded that the Army was not sending something to Will; Will was sending something to Will, in care of Virginia. Will had simply told the Army where to send it and the Army had gotten around to it.

"…and why *Miss* Virginia *Sullivan?* Why not Virginia *Hastings?* Seems like they'd get it right. How is she, anyway? Ain't seen her since, well, the, you know. She at home?"

"Fine, Arnie. She's just fine. Course she's at home; where else would she be?" Poppy smiled again, but with his lips pursed, in a way that showed that Arnie had started to ask too many questions.

Arnie, relieved to find that he was not the agent for Will's corpse and coffin, had simply tried to be sociable. He didn't know what he'd said to ruffle Poppy's feathers, but he knew he had done so, and he felt bad about it. Poppy had a lot on his mind. Everyone counted on him and he had a right to be testy, what with all his worries. Arnie stared at his shoes, scuffed them, to be clear that he had meant no insult.

"Hey, Poppy?" Hoskins had been quiet longer than he liked and, not seeing the shift in Poppy's mood, simply started talking. "Hey, you think Virginia's expectin' it? You know, like a, I don't know, a anniversary present, something like that? Has it been a year? Maybe just one of them things soldiers do? Remember Bradley's boy? He used to send Old Man Bradley stuff when he was stationed there in Hawaii, chopsticks and paper stuff. Bet that's what it is."

Part of the burden of having the sheriff as a partner was putting up with Hoskins being stupid. *Chopsticks and paper things? What an idiot — that box is probably two-and-a-half feet high and deep and three feet long.* Hoskins at least had diverted Arnie's equally dull mind from further questions.

"Don't know, Sheriff. Don't know. But tell ya' what, we need to find out. Do I need to sign anything?" Poppy, facing Arnie, made it clear from his expression that he had no intention of signing anything. He held out the bill of lading. It did not obviously call for a signed receipt but, if it had, Arnie would have been the one to sign it — they all knew that without even saying it.

"Naw, Poppy. Virginia's in your household. You can pick it up for her. That's good enough. You take it. And tell her I said Hidy. Hope she's doin' fine."

"Thanks, Arnie, I will, I will. Sheriff, think you and Arnie might give me a hand?"

The men picked the box up. It was not so heavy that they could tell what was in it. They shook it a bit, heard nothing, then carried it out of the depot, onto the platform, and down the steps where they hefted it onto the pickup bed of the county law enforcement truck.

"Thanks again, Poppy. And when you see Bart, tell 'im I said Hidy to him, too." Arnie thought about asking if Poppy could spare a Lucky Strike, then thought better of it and stepped to one side to let the pickup drive off.

If Arnie had watched he would have seen the sheriff drive back past the burned cotton gin, then steer the pickup south out into the cotton farms instead of back into town. Only the prairie dogs bobbing up and down watched the cloud of dust behind the truck. Before the pickup had gone fifty yards, Hoskins had turned to face Poppy.

"Whatcha wanna do with this here box? You think Virginia's waitin' on it?"

"No, no, I don't think she is. Don't want to surprise her, you know. It isn't Christmas. No, I think we'd better look after what's good for her right now." By that Hoskins knew that Poppy meant to put the box in the shed out by the quarry.

Back in 1937, when Roosevelt paved over the road between Lubbock and Clovis, the engineers had looked for a place with plenty of dirt and limestone and near enough to the road project to pile the material and store the machinery. They found a hollow at the base of a small bluff where a wet weather creek flowed during rains. Roosevelt took it over, carved out a quarry, sent the WPA in to plant trees to keep the dirt from blowing it all away, then abandoned it when the road work was finished.

The quarry was the only place within fifty miles that couldn't be seen from town. A high pampa guarded one side from view and the trees, up on a bluff, blocked the other. After the highway was dedicated and the last road grader disappeared, Poppy printed up some notices that warned against trespassing on U.S. Government Property and nailed them to every fence post on every dirt road leading anywhere near the quarry. He put two padlocks on the abandoned shed and told Hoskins to keep an eye on it. Except for high school kids who went skinny dipping when rain filled the quarry, no one dared come within a mile of the place. They drove up to the shed and turned off the engine.

Poppy unlocked the chains and Hoskins swung open one of the corrugated tin doors. The two men wrestled the box off the pickup bed and into the shed. They had to stand it on one end to get it around everything stacked up inside but, with effort, they successfully wrestled the crate to the one open space they kept for inspecting goods on arrival.

They stood over the box. Hoskins looked at Poppy. Poppy looked back. Even then he thought about packing it back onto the truck, taking it home, and dumping it in Virginia's bedroom. *Serve her right*, he thought to himself. But that was not part of the plan, not the long view.

Hoskins waited. They stood there for a few minutes before Poppy decided. At length he shook his head no. The box was not opened. They shoved it up against the back wall of the shed, then walked out and chained the doors closed.

Hoskins, like Arnie, wasn't exactly sure what he had witnessed but knew it was enough to upset Poppy. *If it ain't that sorry kid of his, it's the girl.* Neither of them said a word about what was in the box as they drove off.

Bart read the entire letter, then read it a second time, turned it over, checked the address, and laughed.

June 1, 1944

Dear Virginia:

A last letter. Well, I hope not, but we've been put in trucks and brought someplace that isn't London and isn't Division...All I can say is that I see boats and water ...Missed Peter in London...

Tell Shirley thanks for the picture...

Shirley's like a boll weevil, Bart thought, *killing what she can't eat.* He had not forgiven Shirley her rejections but he did admire the way she stuck her fork in Virginia. Shirley may have thrown in the towel as far as getting Will for herself but, *This takes the prize, sending him that picture of Virginia.*

It would just be a matter of time before Will figured it out. *Lord let me be there to see the look on her face when he gets home...*

He considered whether to tack the letter on the bulletin board, without even showing it to Poppy, then remembered what his father had said just a day or two ago: *Bart, someone's gonna think you're getting too big for your britches. Stay away from Clovis for a while.* And Virginia had made some snotty remark about the scratch on his forehead, as if she knew anything. Poppy had gone on.

"Do you know anything about Mrs. Tarlton's sugar? Or all that brisket the Reillys and came up with over July Fourth?"

Bart had denied knowing anything.

What Poppy doesn't know won't hurt him, he decided. *I'll decide what goes through the mail.* He put Will's letter with the others, neither realizing nor caring that what Virginia didn't know might hurt her.

Hoskins took up the scratch pad, read it a last time, and called the jailer to come in.

"All right, I been out to the 'dobes. Wasn't nothing to it."

"Didn't figure they was," the jailer said. "Them people just liken to make trouble." The jailer had not been to the labor camp himself, although he had jailed a few of the field hands to sleep off a raging drunk. He agreed with the general notion that they were a hot-blooded bunch of trouble makers when they weren't picking cotton.

"So, what'd you tell the law over in New Mexico?" Hoskins asked.

"Said I'd have you look into it, like I tol' ya."

"Anything else? We supposed to get back to 'em?"

The jailer couldn't remember if he had said yes or no to that.

"Okay, that's all. No, wait. Here's the deal. If they call back tell 'em I went out there, the girl was all right." Hoskins thought for a moment, letting his weak powers of imagination bump along until he came up with a story he could believe. "Nobody said she was raped, nothin' like that, and I sure didn't see no evidence of it." That was true enough; the girl had a few bruises but they weren't from lifting her skirts up. And they hadn't said the word 'rape,' not in any way, shape or form. Nor had she said 'Bart' or 'Sullivan.' "In fact, they kept saying it was some guy named Casero or something like that. So I closed it."

The jailer left. Hoskins tore the jailer's note up and put it in the trash. He wondered how they figured it was Bart — his name wasn't Casero. No matter, he had got out there fast enough to shut them up, and they wouldn't be calling the law again, not any time soon, not unless they got some work cards or something. "Fuckin' wetbacks, more trouble'n they're worth," Hoskins mumbled to himself. "And she wasn't that good lookin." For him, the case was closed.

Bart made sure no one was inside the post office, then opened the special box. He found inside a request for a dozen blue stamps for processed foods. *Someone's wife must be sick,* he figured. There was a request for a Ration Book Four with some of the airplane stamps, not the tank ones. Someone needed a whole sheet of reds or two sheets of browns. *That's a mistake; the meat buyers have already come and gone for the month.* There were the usual requests for shoes, bicycle tires, enough gasoline to drive every car in Tierra to Los Angeles and back. One note demanded enough Number 30's for five pounds of sugar. *What does she do with all that sugar?* And several bottles of Old Crow or Jim Beam, for the sheriff. *Well,* he thought. *This'll take a while. But if some's good, more's better.*

He was certain that Poppy was wrong. When Poppy had said that the invasion of France meant the end of rationing food and gas and prices would fall like a rock, well, Poppy just didn't know what he was talking about. *Old people don't know everything, not by a long shot.*

"So, did you call the sheriff?"

"I did." The two men sat in the examining room, the doctor in the side chair, the cop up on the table. The doctor poured coffee out of a metal pot into ceramic cups. The cop wiped spilled drops off the side of the cup and licked his fingers. The doctor used a sterile towel, or what had once been a sterile towel, to wipe his hand and wrists. He was a good doctor; he was a good cop. Neither of them could have made a living waiting tables.

"And he said?"

"Didn't actually let me talk to the sheriff, said he was on patrol. Anyways, it was like you said it was going to be. Said the sheriff went out there, talked to the people, looked at the girl. Said she wasn't actually raped. Sheriff said whoever got to her turned out to be one of their own people, somebody named Casero. That family must have the place by the neck."

The doctor shook his head, took a sip of coffee, then put the cup down on the counter top where the jars of cotton swabs and Q-tips were lined up next to the Merthiolate and plaster tape. He didn't say anything, just shook his head.

"So, do I owe you a buck?"

"Forget it. It wasn't a fair bet — I knew what was going to happen."

"It wasn't *el casero*, the handyman. It was *el cartero*." The postman. She was a Mexican kid; the man was a gringo, apparently a gringo of some influence over in Texas. This wasn't the first time Dr. Martinez had cleaned up a mess on such a girl that had been caused by such a boy.

"So, what do you want me to do? He shows up out at the State Line every weekend. I can pick him up when he gets on this side of the state line. Or when he leaves the bar. Drunk, disorderly, you know."

"Just keep an eye on him, see if he does something. Don't want him hurting anyone if you can stop it. But I don't think you should just go pick him up. Unless he does something."

"That's it? I mean, you know, he can spend a night or two in my hotel, easy."

"Just if he does something. Otherwise he tells the judge you didn't actually witness him doing anything, not speeding or having a drink or even parking the car, and that's the last we'll see of him. No, unless he does something, that's it." The doctor was firm.

That wasn't it, the cop knew. He didn't know what 'it' would be, but it would be something. *Dr. Martinez is one of those quiet ones, but real smart.* The officer was pretty sure the doctor had a plan, even if the rat lived over the state line in Texas.

"You going to learn how to make coffee some day?"

"I don't know. You going to learn how to drink out of a cup some day?"

"Maybe. You going to stop butchering people some day?"

"Maybe."

"You will tell me when you go after that kid, won't you?"

"Maybe."

CHAPTER EIGHT

August 1944

She felt plump, tired, and increasingly scared. Doc had told her to stay off her feet, then told her she needed to walk. "'Goddamnit,' he had said, "when I told you to stay off your feet, you were workin' on the second floor of the courthouse. When'd they fire you? A month ago? Two months ago? So what'd you think I meant? Go home and eat? Go get some exercise."

She had only gained about fifteen pounds, a change in girth that every woman in Tierra clucked over. *Too thin, that girl,* one said. *Baby'll be sickly, you watch. It's not like she can't eat anything she wants,* another said, alluding to the general belief that Poppy could provide Virginia with all the steaks and milk and cheese and anything else she might want, war or no.

She had taken to walking to the newspaper twice a day. The smell of printer's ink in the morning made her sick to her stomach. The clatter of the Babcock press and its flying ink slung from a faulty tray gave her a headache. But she hadn't received a single letter since before the invasion, before "D-Day" they called it, and the Texas press wire service was at Poppy's newspaper office. Regardless of what Poppy said, she didn't believe he would tell her if bad news came.

Since D-Day she had studied the map of France, or at least the map of Northern France. The radio and the MovieTone news at the motion picture show duly reported that the troops had landed on four beaches somewhere north of Paris and were driving the Germans back. She had gone to the county library, gotten an atlas, and found Caen and Bayeux. Weeks later she was still consulting the atlas, searching for Colleville and Cherbourg. In July she began to trace the tiny red road lines between St. Mere Eglise north to Cherbourg, then south again to Valognes.

She was not alone; the town had sprung a fountain of students on the place names of Normandy because everyone wanted to know where Will was. *Heard anything? Bet he's around back in the rear; that's where they always put the medics.* She didn't know. *Hope he weren't at St. Mare Eagles?* She didn't know. *Wonder if they've got him with them fellers on the way to Carentan. Lot of fightin' around there.* To each of them she confessed that she had no more news than they had, not of Will and not of anyone else. The town worried with her.

In the middle of July Mr. Reilly asked her "if Will was in that bunch headed to St. Lô?" This was a new name. She left her groceries and went back to the library where she saw that it was on the other side of the River Vire from Coutances. From the Lubbock newspapers, the radio, and the atlas she soon figured out that the troops were on both sides of the river, one army driving toward Carentan and Coutances, the other attacking St. Lô. This succeeded only in making her worry about two places instead of one.

Day by day she walked into the *Times* where Poppy looked up from his desk. He invariably shook his head to indicate that he had no news; she invariably ignored him and pulled the news wire feeds out of the trash box to read for herself. She began with the casualty lists, then searched for battle reports, staying until the place made her sick or crazy.

• •

/// OWI/// Washington 20Jun44 ///

The Secretary has released the following names to the Associated Press. Local news organizations should confirm with families before publication.

Texas:

.....

Davis, Robert, Abernathy, KIA

Eckhardt, Eldon, Jericho, KIA

Kotram, Wayne, Conway, Missing

Muncy, Joe, Lelia Lake, WIA

Ollinger, Ralph, Goodnight, KIA

And so the war in Europe inched its way toward Tierra County. The O'Donnell's oldest son was on a destroyer that was hit by a German shore gun; Reverend Crater put them on a prayer list. On June 15 the Brittens received a telegram informing them that Derrell had been wounded on the second day; Father O'Malley convened a special mass for his family. One of the Harrell cousins, who lived closer to Littlefield than Tierra, was missing. "We're were pretty sure he didn't make it because all the other boys in his unit was kilt." Virginia knew them all.

Of Hastings there was neither letter nor wire news. "He's fine, just fine. If he wasn't, I'd have got it on the newswire." She didn't believe Poppy.

"No news is good news," Mrs. Fleming told her. "Even Shirley says so," she added, assuming that this would bolster Virginia's spirits. Mrs. Fleming had stopped by to bring a few things. "And how's your mother, dear? Have you been to see her lately?"

Virginia had walked unevenly to answer the knock at the door, let her in, and was relieved to see that Shirley had not come with her mother. She had seen Shirley once or twice at church, at the movies, but they had not spoken in weeks. Only Shirley's mother could be ignorant of the fact that the two girls, who had grown up playing together every day, had come to detest one another.

"I haven't been able to go for about two months now. When I was over there at the start of summer she was just fine."

"Must break your heart. And there's not a thing they can do, is there?"

"No, Ma'am. Not a thing. She just sits there and looks so normal, even looks you in the face and smiles, but never says a word."

"Makes me want to cry. Do they even know what it is?"

"No, Ma'am. They just say she drifted off."

"How does she look?"

Virginia had been heart-broken at her last trip to Lubbock. Apart from looking as if she had entered the wrong room, Emma Sullivan appeared normal. She dressed herself, fed herself, and sat on the edge of her bed from morning until bed time, smiling, leaving only when one of the attendants took her to eat or to walk to the day room. Virginia had given up riding the Greyhound to Lubbock after she entered her seventh month. Poppy had not been to see his wife in more than a year. Bart had never gone.

"Don't you just know she'd love being a grandmother? Have you told her? Well, let's not talk about that, let's talk about you. How are you?"

Virginia had a fear that her mother wasn't really demented. As she had done on the lonely bus rides, she lay awake some nights wondering if it was just a matter of something going wrong in her mother's wiring. Maybe, she thought, her mother had a fully functional mind, that she understood every word that was said, that she was just as alert as when they used to go to church or to Reilly's to buy the week's groceries, but something just kept her from being able to say anything and from being able to show expressions.

She wanted to tell her mother about the baby, even about Poppy having announced that she had eloped with Will, that she had been let go at the courthouse, but she was afraid to. Doc had told them over and over to not upset Emma, that it might set her back. That Virginia had been fired as the ration clerk probably wouldn't mean a thing to Emma; she had been in the hospital long before Virginia got the job at the courthouse. There had been no rationing then, nor even a war, back when Emma had been taken away from home. And as for the baby, she didn't know what she could say to her mother about it, and decided to not try.

"I'm fine, Mrs. Fleming. I really am."

"You ought to be due any time." Mrs. Fleming could count nine months from Thanksgiving as well as anyone else. "Have you got everything ready? It must be pretty hard with your husband over there. Is anybody helpin' you? I'll bet Shirley would do anything for you. Do you need anything?"

Virginia needed a lot of things. A baby bed. More bottles. More clothes. More diapers. A doctor. A mother.

Virginia remembered having wished a few days before high school graduation that she were Shirley. Mr. Fleming and Mrs. Fleming had driven Shirley over to Lubbock for a day in the city, and Virginia had been invited. Mr. Fleming had parked next to the First Bank of Lubbock. "I'll be an hour," he had said. Mrs. Fleming and Shirley waited for Virginia to get out of the car, then started off walking away down a sidewalk, a paved sidewalk, as if they went there every day. At the corner Mrs. Fleming held Virginia back a moment. "Wait 'til it's green, those cars will stop." They walked another block, then paused in front of a shop. In the window there were four mannequins, each with styled wigs. Two wore April dresses. Another, partially covered by a thick towel, was dressed in a black swimsuit. The fourth was draped in a wedding gown. Mrs. Fleming and Shirley chattered about the sleeves, the collars, giggled at the swimsuit. They walked on to the FedWay and, without even stopping to look in the window, walked right in through the double glass doors. The three women passed through rows of ladies clothing racked on hangers, a department of smart shoes, women's coats on sale, and entered a small restaurant at the rear of the store. The chairs, the linoleum, the counter tops, all were in patent black and the tables had chrome legs. They sat the way women sat at fancy restaurants in the movies. A Negro woman served iced tea to them and Shirley ordered pecan pie. "Would you like some pie, Virginia?" Mrs. Fleming had asked. Virginia did, but she had no purse and even if she had brought a purse there would have been no more than a few pennies in it. "No, ma'am," she had said, wishing she had been able to turn to the black woman and say yes, she would like a piece of pecan pie. They talked of graduation, of Hoyt and Johnny saying they might just up and join the army, of how grown up they all were. Shirley had hummed, *I've Got You Under My Skin*. Mrs. Fleming paid, then left ten cents on the table for the black woman. They walked back to the car along different streets, passing a sheet music shop, a pharmacy with nylons and lipsticks displayed in the window, and a shop which sold only women's hats. To Virginia's relief, they did not enter any of them.

"I hope I'm not late," Mr. Fleming said when he came out of the bank. He started up the Buick, then drove along Broadway before turning down a street Virginia had never seen before. Broad lawns, enormous buildings with high glass windows, Southern mansions dotted the blocks. It was the technological college. "Can we just drive though, Daddy?" Shirley had asked. Without another word Mr. Fleming steered through the campus. "Will you be going to college?" Mrs. Fleming turned to ask Virginia. Virginia detected Mr. Fleming's signal, a slight quick turn of his head, eyes darting, and when Virginia said that she would not, Mrs. Fleming did not pursue the question. Virginia thought perhaps they had invited her along so that they could stop by the hospital to see her mother, but the Buick didn't go anywhere near the south side of the city. Mr. Fleming instead invited them for chicken fried steak at a café near the new air field and, after eating, they drove all the way back to Tierra. It had seemed so normal.

That night, at home, Virginia had asked Poppy if he knew that Shirley was going to college. She had not asked for anything at home, not since Emma had been taken to the state hospital. He had said that he knew it. That was as close as Virginia came to going to college. Now she was pregnant, alone, and still talking to Mrs. Fleming.

"I don't have hardly anything lined up. Poppy was going to take me to Lubbock but something came up. He'll take me soon, maybe this weekend."

"By 'hardly anything,' what do you mean?" Mrs. Fleming was no midwife, but given how little weight Virginia had gained, she would not have been surprised to see the girl go into labor right then. "Clothes?"

"Well, not much. Not anything, really."

"Diapers? Bottles? And who's going to get the house ready?"

"What do you mean, get the house ready?"

She meant 'clean,' but didn't want to say it quite that way.

"Well, you're going to be down a week or more. Wherever you're going to take care of this baby, well, the house has got to be fixed up so that you don't get sick from anything, you or the baby either." She wondered whether Doc had told Virginia anything about the eminence of labor, the breaking of water and enemas to ease labor contractions. She couldn't remember a baby being born in town since long before the war started.

"There have to be window screens in the baby's room so it can get fresh air that doesn't have all this dust in it. I never wanted to see another drop of rain but now that this baby's coming and it's dry, well, the dust can be bad. And a crib. You've got to have a crib so that it gets fresh air and doesn't roll over on itself. And no cats."

"We don't keep a cat."

"And a special pan for baths. Not what you cook in, but something you can keep clean."

Shirley's mother was pleased with herself. It had been twelve years since Butch was born and she had called it quits on pregnancies. Even so, memories of diaper buckets, baby dresses, cotton swabs and mucus, boiling rubber nipples and bottles, all had come flooding back. As she spoke she decided that she would get the Ladies Bible Class to do something, a baby shower maybe, or fix up some old things they had at home. When she satisfied herself that she had told Virginia all she needed to know and had a plan for what she didn't know, she got up to leave.

"Oh, dear me, I nearly forgot. I came to bring this to you and we got to talking and I...." She handed a thin sleeve of an envelope to Virginia. It was not a letter but, instead, had a pinked cut across the top and was rather stiff. "Shirley said you should have this, that you would want it. Isn't she thoughtful!"

Virginia took it, opened it, and almost fell.

Mrs. Fleming was past paying attention to Virginia.

"I don't know who took that picture. It is a nice picture and you look just like you but I think they got Will out of focus. But it's just precious! Is he all right? We don't hear anything. We're all thinking of him. Where is he? Do you know?"

Mrs. Fleming's question was the one too many and for the first time in memory, Virginia began to cry.

"I don't know. I don't know where he is." She tried to tell her that Peter was over there too, but great globs of snot and tears blocked her throat and she trailed off before the words got out. Mrs. Fleming put her arm around her the way Emma would have done if Emma were home and not crazy, then wiped her face with a kitchen towel. "I haven't gotten a letter since before the invasion. I go every day to check but...."

Mrs. Fleming shushed and shooed her from blubbering out painful things.

"You can't help it. It'll be all right. He'll be fine." Even Mrs. Fleming didn't believe much of what she said, particularly to the degree that it required faith in getting the mail. She hadn't approved Bart putting letters up on the post office wall, not that she boycotted them; at least she thought it had been wrong. Mrs. Fleming did not perceive that it was after Bart had gotten so sick last Spring that Virginia had stopped receiving letters; as did most, she assumed only that Virginia now read her letters in private. "It's the war."

And there Mrs. Fleming left her.

Oh my God, I'm really alone in this. I don't care about Ladies Bible Classes or car rides to Lubbock or window screens. Virginia was indeed alone. For the first time she questioned her decision. *Maybe you are just like all those girls they talk about — 'oh she just got swept up in the war' — you wanted to send your soldier away with something to remember and now you're pregnant and alone.*

But Virginia had not slept around in haste to repent at leisure. She had made the deliberate decision to get on the bus herself, to follow him and find him before he got on the train that would take him to the place where the army collected the men and sent them off in boats to go to the war. She had made it clear that she wanted to be alone with him in a bedroom and open up herself to him and take him to her for her own sake, without regret, without apology, and without explanation, and she had done it. He hadn't demanded it, almost hadn't even agreed to it, but she made it clear that she would have him and if it came to pass, she would have his baby, just in case the war didn't bring him back to her. This was no case of hysteria driven by war and separation — she had made that bargain with herself first and then with him. She had been ripe and she had exhausted both of them, and then he had been taken away. It had been her decision, and that he had vanished in the days when the army stormed ashore in France proved to her that she had been right to want to keep that much of him behind inside her.

Before she put it with the locket she kept hidden in her drawer she looked once more at the photograph. *He's not out of focus. That's just the way he looked.* She caught herself, already speaking of him in the past tense. But, in her heart, she knew that he was dead.

CHAPTER NINE

August 15, 1944

"Give me a fag."

Butch liked to call them fags. Sluggo called them 'cigs.' Tommy and Sandy referred to them as smokes. No one actually called them cigarettes. Finding one was a treat; finding a Lucky Strike was a miracle. In 1944 the only way to get a Lucky Strike was out of a box of Army rations or take one from the next guy over in the foxhole. The guys were suitably impressed.

"Where'd you get this?"

"Ah, just found it."

"Yeah, bull. You stole it."

"Did not. Found it."

"Liar. Give me one."

"Me too."

Tommy turned to hide whatever it was he had them in, drew four out, passed them around. They all took one. A match was struck. The boys lit up.

"Nothing like a Lucky for flavor," Butch said with an air of experience.

"Better taste, cooler smoke."

"That's Chesterfields. Don't you know anything?"

"Steady nerves!"

"Camels. *You want steady nerves to launch a tin fish. Or make one.* They all admired the Camel advertisement, a cluster of sailors smoking inside a submarine.

They inhaled and exhaled and let the pungent smoke swirl around their nostrils as they gazed across the cotton fields from the platform of the windmill high above Tommy's family farm. The smoke drifted, evaporated.

"No kidding. Where'd you find these? Come on."

Butch made a deal.

"We're the American army now — me and Tommy. You're the Nazis."

"No way."

"Okay, not our problem. You want to bum off us…"

Sluggo wasn't so sure. They hadn't played army for months, anyway. The rain had wrecked the first part of the summer and now that it was gone everyone, except Butch, was working. "Like the wetbacks," Butch reminded them. Tommy worked for his dad. Sluggo cleaned the offal from his uncles' slaughterhouse. Sandy had given up all of his jobs in town to work in the fields when they were dry although, on Sundays, after church he went over to the Sullivans to see if Virginia needed anything. Now that the fields were wet again he was looking for lawns to mow and haunting Old Bradley's barber shop.

"Okay. You're Americans. We're the Japs. Where'd you find 'em?"

The rain had poured so much water into the ground that the scrawny creek bed that wound past the cemetery and on toward the quarry was full of water.

"Follow me," Butch had said, and shimmied down the steel legs of the windmill. Sluggo and Sandy followed and they took off walking across the muddy cotton fields to the bluff overlooking the quarry a half mile away.

"We goin' swimmin'? The quarry's full of water."

"Like there's a box of Lucky Strikes in the water? Are you stupid or what?"

"Could be. Remember Captain Blood? He found a box of treasure under the ocean."

"Sea Hawk. Not Captain Blood."

"Not Captain Blood. Count of Monte Christo. And it was in a cave."

"No. But you're gettin' warm."

They came up to the barbed wire fence at the top of the bluff. Poppy's phony 'No Trespassing — U.S. Government' signs were still nailed to the fence posts, albeit faded. They crawled through the fence and into the tree line at the top of the bluff. Through the trees they looked down on the quarry. It was about thirty yards long and half as wide, formed by the bluff on one side and a rock outcrop on the other side. The creek, no more than an erosion scar most of the year, trickled water in at the northerly end. The opposite end had been closed by a dirt dam built by the Corps of Engineers.

The quarry was brimming with water. The few clouds in the sky reflected from its flat surface, the tops of the trees where the boys lay hidden were mirrored on the water. At the deep end a large boulder emerged, a rock so large and flat that it was known by every kid in Tierra as 'the diving rock,' a stone from which all of them had jumped, dived, fallen, and taken naps when they sneaked away from home to swim.

The shed, on the opposite side of the quarry, was big enough to hold several pickups. Its flat walls were made from cheap plywood, windowless, and capped by a tin gabled roof that reflected the hot August sun. The doors were on the other side, away from the quarry and away from the boys.

"Okay, Hot Shot. Now what?"

Butch led them single file down the short bluff face to the edge of the quarry. Water lapped at their feet as they walked along the soft dirt near the bluff, the pool opening up to their left as they bounced and hopped along the path toward the earthen dam. It was a place they all knew. They crossed the narrow dam on foot, jumped down near the shed, and followed Butch as he trotted the last few yards. They walked along the west wall to the corner and stopped.

"There." Butch pointed to the tar paper that had fallen away from the wall. Years of wind and battering revealed the two-inch by twelve-inch planks that made up the wall.

"So I come out here the other day to take a swim and walked over here to pee and — look!" He pointed to a loose board on one corner. "I thought, well that board might make a decent diving board, and I was gonna just pull it off and take it out to the divin' rock and so I started pryin' on it. I got it to where it was loose enough to open enough for me to squeeze through and I thought I'd get inside and push it off from in there."

As he spoke he folded the tar paper away and, sure enough, there was a two-by-twelve plank, the lower end warped by wind and rain and jutting away from the corner of the shed. Butch got down on his knees and began to tug on the board which began to open away from the rest of the wall. Tommy got down on his knees and pulled on the other edge of the plank; it slowly began to open up, the nails creaking as the board pressed against them. When the space was big enough for a tight squeeze, Butch put his head in the gap, then his shoulders, then slipped out of view. He was in.

One by one the treasure hunters squeezed in through the boards, stood up on the dirt floor, and bumped into the boxes and machines that were stacked about near the corner. They squinted, blinked, and adjusted their vision and, not two feet from the opening, saw a big, open cardboard box, a box with a Lucky Strike sign on the side. More full than empty, the box was big enough to hold fifty or a hundred cartons of cigarettes. Five more boxes, Chesterfields, Camels, Kools, were stacked on the same pallet.

"This is my stash," Butch declared. "When I need a fag, this is where I come."

They gaped at the find. Lucky Strikes, and every other cigarette advertised in the *Saturday Evening Post*, were as rare as hen's teeth. It was common knowledge that the only way to get a pack was to be in the army. Yet here in front of them was neither a pack nor a carton but a whole pallet of the things.

"And I call dibs. It's mine," Butch continued. "But I share."

He reached inside, took a carton, and began to open it to divide right there in the shed.

"Two for you, two for you,…"

"Easier to keep 'em all together. We can split 'em up back in town," Sandy proposed. "Let's see what else is here."

Seeing what else was there was not easy or certain. The big swinging front doors were closed and, they knew from experience, locked with chains and padlocks. There were no windows. But through the cracks in the planks, through beams of light filtered with dust motes, a picture of the contents began to emerge.

"Look at this," Tommy pointed. Against the back wall there were stacks of tires, new tires, still wrapped in paper. There were big tires for pickups, smaller tires for cars, and even some very thin tires that could only be for bicycles. "We can get these tires over to Homer and make a fortune."

"Hell, sell 'em ourselves."

"What are you gonna do, put a sign on the highway? New tires?"

"Maybe. Why not?"

"What are you gonna tell 'em? Found 'em?"

There were cases of motor oil on a pallet. Cases of leather shoes. A crate of nails. A tarp covered a dozen drums of gasoline. Boxes of sugar. Boxes of canned fruit.

"What's that?" Sluggo pointed to a rusty machine in the opposite corner.

"Dunno. A motor of some kind. Big one. See all the flywheels and compression chambers?" He pointed out the various tubes and hoses which connected the parts of the large industrial engine.

It was the only thing that wasn't new.

The boys' gaze lifted and, for no apparent reason, they began to whisper.

"Hey — whose stuff is this?"

"I dunno. Why?"

"I'll tell you whose — it's the government's. That's why they've got those signs on the fences."

"Why do they want it? And why'd they put it out here? Seems like they'd keep it at an army base, or in Lubbock."

"I don't know. Maybe it's reserves."

It then occurred to them that they were not finding. They were stealing.

"Put the fags back and let's get out of here."

"Yeah. Let's get."

Butch looked at the open Lucky Strike box, then at the carton he had begun to share, then back at the box, and made a very bad decision.

"It was already open. Someone's comin' out here for cigarettes and they don't miss what I took. I'm keepin' these."

"Let's scram."

It was when the last of them got out through the plank that they heard a pickup truck driving right up to the front of the shed. Their hearts froze in place.

"Stop!" Butch hissed. He held up his hand in warning, then turned his palm down and motioned toward the ground rapidly, three times. The boys all jumped to the ground and stretched out flat. The engine sputtered to a stop in front of the shed and, soon, the squeak of a door handle was followed by the thud of a tin pickup door slammed shut. They could not see the shed doors but they could hear someone open the padlocks, rattle the chains, and swing the doors wide open and around to the sides of the building.

"Let's get out of here," Butch whispered.

"What if they catch us?"

"If we stay here we'll sure find out." And with that, Sandy tiptoed away, directly to the earth dam, then crouched low to sneak across it. Each of the boys followed, breath held, fear permeating every step. When Tommy finally reached the west end of the dam they scrambled into the trees and from there up the bluff. At last Sandy stopped, laid down on his stomach, and hid behind an elm tree. The others dropped to the ground.

"Look."

Not thirty yards away, right where they had been at the corner of the shed, a stocky man in a cowboy hat and boots, a man with a mustache and a star on his chest, stood and glared at the quarry. He put his hands on his hips, spread his legs, and stared directly at them, unable to see because of the glare of the five o'clock sun and the growth of WPA elms.

No one said a word, or even breathed.

The sheriff stared at the bluff, then slowly swivelled to his left to focus across the pasture in the direction of the Carter farm a mile away. He turned back and peered to the north in the general direction of town and along the dirt ruts he had just driven to get to the shed. It seemed to them that he looked right at them. Suddenly he put his hands up to his face and shouted:

"Who the hell's out there?"

Sluggo nearly answered but Sandy, quicker, clapped his hand over Sluggo's mouth.

Hoskins waited.

"If there's anybody up there you're in some serious goddamned trouble. Get your ass down here."

They were all tempted to get up but before any of them stood, Hoskins turned and gazed again across the scrub and dirt between the shed and the barbed wire fence at the edge of the Carter land, barely visible in the distance. He was facing directly away from them.

"I said if there's anybody out there, you're under arrest. Come here, goddamn you."

He waited but no one came. The boys stayed on their stomachs.

"Shhh. He don't know we're here," Butch hissed.

"Shut up. He'll hear you," Sandy hissed back.

"How's he gonna catch us? We're up here, he's down there."

They waited several minutes, as did Hoskins. Nothing happened. At length the sheriff walked back out of view to the front of the shed. They held their breath. Several moments later they saw the outline of the north door swing closed and shortly, there was the sound of a groaning starter and a sputtering engine. A cloud of oil choked out of the tail pipe, followed by the clash of badly shifted gears. The county law enforcement vehicle backed up, turned around, and drove away from the shed, going east on the ruts across the pasture and as far away from the hiding boys as it was possible to do.

"To the fence." It was time to leave.

The boys held their collective breath until the last of the dust raised by the disappearing truck had settled and no sign of the vehicle was left. When no speck of any kind was visible on the horizon, they stood and, to their surprise found that they were shaking.

"Butch?"

"Yeah?"

"You're a dumbass. A real dumbass," Sandy said.

"How'd I know someone would be out there?"

"No, Dumbass. It ain't that you'd know if anybody'd be out there. It's who was out there that makes you stupid."

"Piss on you."

"Piss on you, Dumbass. You come this close to gettin' all of us in the same trouble you're in."

"What's that if you're so damned smart?"

"You wasn't just stealin' fags. You was stealin' fags from the sheriff."

"Let's get out of here."

"Vamoos."

They vamoosed under the barbed wire fence and back across the cotton fields, running, stopping, looking to see if they were being chased. They circled around the cemetery, slowly, to see whether Hoskins was waiting with handcuffs, chains, a shotgun, dogs, whatever a sheriff might use to nab a bunch of shed thieves.

He wasn't.

When they got close to town Tommy said they should skirt around behind the courthouse for fear that Hoskins might be standing in front of the jail on the corner, waiting for them.

"Maybe he just let us do his job for him. Why nab us out there when we had to come home? He could just wait and arrest us here. I'll bet that's what he's doing, just waitin' for us.

"Bull! He didn't see nothin'. He never looked up. And even if he did, from down there he wouldn't know who we was anyway," Butch protested.

They biked to the street that separated Nona's from the Magnolia Station, then got off the bikes and pushed them to the edge of the vacant lot.

"You got to get rid of those fags, Butch. Even if they don't arrest us now, if somebody finds you with a bunch of Luckies there ain't but one place you could have got 'em. Soon as somebody tells Hoskins that you've got Luckies he'll come get you." Sandy had a fair point.

Butch never got in any trouble or, more correctly, as the banker's son when he did get in trouble the consequences were negligible, being told to stay in his room for an hour, getting only half his dessert, having to take the trash out. Even so, the idea that he might be fingered by the sheriff was enough to make him pause. It dawned on Sandy and even on Butch, to a lesser degree, that the shed was full of things that people couldn't get at the store. Franklin's was out of nails, but they came up with some. Mrs. Tarlton was out of sugar, but she always seemed to find a bag. Sandy's mother never had a roast or a ham but on July Fourth the tables on the courthouse lawn had been covered with barbeque.

The four conspirators grew quiet. Since it was late on a Sunday they would have to disperse anyway, some for supper, some for church, all for baths. They edged toward the lengthening shadows of the elms that bordered the west end of the lot when a *scusshhh* of air brakes made them turn to look behind.

The Greyhound braked, downshifted, and then turned off the highway between Nona's and the filling station. Its front tires skidded on the gravel street, then straightened out and pointed in the direction of the town square. The bus rarely stopped in town. Few people got on it and fewer still seemed to get off, and when they did, there was a signal arm on a pole at the Magnolia Station to let the driver know someone in Tierra was waiting. For a Greyhound to turn off the highway and drive into town was occasion enough for them to turn and look at it.

And, for there to be a soldier, a real, live soldier, in a green Army uniform and necktie and a cap on his shoulder, sitting in the front row, that was enough to make them forget about Sheriff Hoskins. They jumped on their bikes, bounced across the lot, and made it to the town square just as the bus door opened.

The soldier stepped down to the street, turned, and reached back into the open bus door. With a heave he hauled down his army bag, big enough to stuff any of the boys into and heavy enough that even he had to strain to pull the strap over his shoulder and swing the bag onto his back. He called up to the driver, said thanks, and waved as the door closed. When he turned around, he found the four boys, gaping, eyes wide open, staring at him from over the handlebars of their American Flyers.

"Hi," he said. He sort of smiled, polite but in a bashful way. "Who are you?"

They fumbled around, surprised he would ask, or care, but told him their names. Sluggo. Sandy. Tommy. Butch, Butch Fleming.

"You're Shirley's little brother, aren't you?"

"Yeah," the little felon beamed. "I'm not her little brother, though. I'm nearly as tall as she is."

"I can see that. You sure did get big fast." With his free hand he reached out and shook Butch's hand, then the others'.

"Well, good. Listen, I've got to go. I got to find a phone and tell my folks I'm here. So, tell her I said hi, okay?"

"Okay. Sure I will. You bet I will. Oh, who are you?"

"Hoyt. Hoyt Carter. Guess wouldn't any of you remember me. I've been gone a long time."

CHAPTER TEN

August 15, 1944

The return of Hoyt Carter was an occasion to rejoice.

His mother thought his telephone call was a prank. Mr. Carter told whomever it was to stop bothering them. It wasn't until Hoyt said, "No, Daddy, it's me. It's really me," did Mr. Carter himself collect, then lose, his bearings and begin to fall, a tumble interrupted only by the fact that Hoyt's own younger brother, Jim Ned, had grown big enough to catch his father by the arm. Nell, thirteen, heard his scratchy voice through the telephone mouthpiece, had enough presence of mind to catch it, and heard Hoyt say "Daddy? Daddy? Are you all right?" Mrs. Carter did faint, briefly, and by the time she wrestled the phone back Jim Ned was looking for the salts and Mr. Carter was spluttering in tongues. The first communication between family and son was, "Hoyt? Is it really you?" and, "I'm at the sheriff's here at the courthouse. Do you think you could get the truck out and come down here to get me?"

In the meantime Sluggo and Tommy had raced home on their bicycles to tell their families that they had met a soldier named Hoyt. Sandy told his mother who in turn, ran next door to the church and repeated it to the first person she saw. Mrs. Tarlton reported the news to Reverend Crater who promptly led the congregation in prayer, suspended services and joined the rush to the town square. Poppy heard the news and came with Virginia. Tommy pointed out to Sandy and Sluggo that Butch had come back with his father. The boys hid behind the grownups to stay out of Sheriff Hoskins' view. Miss Somerville at the telephone exchange rang all the party lines and a small procession of farmers and ranchers raced into town to witness the miracle of the boy who had got away from the Japanese. By the time the Carters arrived to collect their son nearly everyone in Tierra had arrived.

The town tried to take Hoyt away from the Carters that evening and might have done so if Hoyt hadn't turned around and said to them:

"I thank ya for comin' but I really need to go home with my folks." Jim Ned had shouldered Hoyt's barracks bag onto the pickup. Mr. and Mrs. Carter hugged on each other and on Hoyt as they scrummed out the door and across the courthouse lawn to their truck. Hoyt held them both with one arm and held Nell with the other as they made away.

The only ones missing, it seemed, were Shirley, who was at home and stretched out on her bed, and Bart.

And Old Bradley, Johnny's father. No one had thought to go tell the barber that his missing son's life-long friend had made it home from war.

It was on Tuesday, ten days after Hoyt came home, that Tommy saw the green sedan.

The drab olive Packard had not been seen in Tierra much that summer. There had been whispers and nervous jokes after July Fourth: the Sangers, who owned the butcher shop, and Reilly, the grocer, had covered the tables on the courthouse lawn with enough brisket and pork ribs to exhaust the rations of a town three times the size of Tierra. The gallons of real ice cream flowing in buckets and jars sated the sweet tooth of every child in the county. Many worried that word of the town's flagrant disregard of meat quotas and the consumption of dairy products otherwise destined for the army would get back to the nosy G-men at their office in Lubbock, but until that Tuesday in mid-August, none had come. By then all had forgotten July Fourth. Few remembered that Virginia's ration desk had been audited regularly right up until the day when Judge Oaks let her go because she was too pregnant to safely walk up the courthouse stairs. Fewer still even knew that the green car had been parked outside Mr. Fleming's bank one day early in the summer.

So, when Tommy saw it parked at the jail, he knew why it was there.

"Number One — it was parked at the jail. Number two — Hoskins runs the jail. Number three — Hoskins saw us."

"If Hoskins had seen us he wouldn't have waited till now," Butch argued. "My dad dragged me back down to the square that night Hoyt Carter came home and I figured right then we was done for." Butch's point should have given them peace of mind — they had all been right there at the jail that night and no one had come to get them. Afterward, in the way conspirators have, they had avoided each other. They had not played army on the intervening Sunday, nor hit grounders, nor smoked on anyone's windmill platform. But when Tommy's father drove into town to buy farm supplies at Franklin's the first thing Tommy saw was the green car parked outside the courthouse.

"You be back here in fifteen minutes, hear?"

Tommy heard. He told his father he would, then ran as fast as he could to Butch's house. He told Butch, in three points, that the government men were in town, then walked slowly back to meet his father and await his arrest.

Butch was indecisive. He preferred hiding in his room to going out of the house to find Sandy and Sluggo. However, by two in the afternoon he had read his old comic books twice too often, weary of The Human Torch and bored with Captain America. By three he had guessed that if anyone knew where to find Mr. Fleming's son, it was the G-men; they hadn't come, so he guessed that they weren't coming.

He found Sandy at Mr. Grundy's, next to the school building, pushing a rotary mower back and forth over Mr. Grundy's unusually abundant grass.

"Hey."

"Hey. Listen here."

Butch explained the urgency of the problem, then sat under Mr. Grundy's tree and watched Sandy nick and gouge the remainder of the ragged little lawn until he was satisfied that he was done.

They ran all the way to the slaughterhouse, then hung around out back by the unloading chute until Sluggo came out.

"Jesus! You look like a murderer. You have to wear a rubber apron?"

"You know what a dead pig looks like? Or a cow?" Sluggo bent over a faucet and screwed on a rubber water hose, then began to wash down a cement slab in front of the livestock chute. "One shot to the head and pow! Dead. Fall to the floor. Then they put this hook in there," he went on, pointing to his throat, "and drag 'em over to the butcher room. And all the way over there is a trail of blood. Blood and shit. Did you know that as soon as the animal dies it shits? And pisses too."

"You're gonna shit too. The G-men are over talkin' to Hoskins."

By the time Tommy had explained it to Butch, and Butch had explained it to Sandy, then enlarged it for Sluggo's benefit, the G-men were reportedly seeking the boys by name, knew exactly what had been stolen from the government, and would charge them with breaking and entering, theft of government propery, and evading arrest.

"They're gonna take us to Lubbock and put us in federal jail."

"If it was Army property, it's treason."

"You dumbass. Why the hell did you take us out there anyway?"

"Dumbass yourself. Because you wanted me to, d'you forget? 'Hey, show us where you got the fags, Butch. Take us to get some cigarettes, Butch.'"

"They can't arrest us for that."

"For breakin' and enterin'? For stealing government property?"

The mess they were sketching for themselves was comparable to the mess they were standing in. The slab underneath the cattle chute was itself an abattoir of frightened animal leavings, a viscous puddle of red, brown, and yellow offal. They knew they were deep in it and not one of them could think of anything that would shift the blame or reduce their certain imprisonment.

"Hey, Sluggo? How hard is this job anyway? Jesus, it stinks. And the blood and shit."

"I hate it. We been runnin' thirty, forty cows a day through here. And pigs. I never dreamed there was so much meat. I'm thinkin' of becoming a vegetarian."

"Seems like a lot. Where do they all go?"

"Oh, just Reilly's, mostly. Sometimes a rancher'll bring in a couple of head, we'll slaughter 'em and butcher 'em, he'll come pick it up. Nona's Café gets a lot of hamburgers. Never knew a town could eat so much meat. I thought we was supposed to be rationing."

"Rationing at my house, that's for sure," Sandy added. "We never have enough coupons for anything and Reilly never has…" He stopped. He had been stocking and delivering groceries for Reilly's for months. When he saw people buy the roast and pork chops and steaks one at a time, it didn't seem like much. When he thought about it, though, Reilly always had enough to sell whatever people asked for, and they always had stamps. Everybody except his mother. It wasn't fair.

No one came to the butcher shop to arrest them. At six o'clock Sluggo's uncle called him to mop up the last of the day's blood and Sandy and Butch slipped out past the loading chutes and down an alley. After five minutes of hiding from block to block they popped out behind Franklin's Hardware. The courthouse was in plain view, but the green sedan wasn't.

They crossed the alley over to the block of buildings where Poppy ran the *Times*. From there they could see across the square to the bank and the grocery store. The green sedan wasn't visible from there either.

"It's gone. We're in the clear."

"Unless it's just gone to arrest us at home. See — Hoskin's truck is gone too. He's probably just showin''em where we live."

Sandy's house was closer to the school; Butch lived farther toward the west end of the town in a two-story home framed by elm trees. They spit on a rock, flipped it, and Sandy guessed "gob" instead of "dry." Butch picked Sandy's house. By resorting to alleys and sprinting across dusty streets they arrived just as Mrs. Clayton walked out onto the front porch.

"Where've you boys been? People have been looking for you."

Sandy's mind raced. This was the moment he feared — telling his mother. It was easy to envision prison, all bars and tin cups and harmonicas. It was harder to explain what trouble he had got into and somehow not make it sound so bad. He never had been able to work out what to say. He just stood there.

"Hello Butch. How's your mother?" She turned to Sandy again. "I said you might be back at Reilly's, I didn't know what you were doing after mowing. He waited a while, then left. You've got no one to blame but yourself. I told him you'd be back for supper, but he said he had other business."

"I've got to go," Butch said.

"Yeah."

"See ya."

"See ya."

Mrs. Clayton put a hand on Sandy's shoulder and turned him to walk up the stoop. He stopped and looked back toward town, watching Butch disappear in a bit of broken field running as he made zigs and zags for the nearest alley. Sandy figured it would be no time before he saw Butch again, and Tommy and Sluggo too.

"So, I've got some ice tea. And corn and some peas. And a surprise."

He didn't quite catch what she was saying, his thoughts tending more to handcuffs, even chains.

"How would you like a steak?"

"A steak?"

"Yes. A nice one, too. I was in Reilly's and waited for you there, too. Anyway, he gave me two steaks, said they had too many and had to get rid of some. He asked if I thought you'd like a nice little T-bone for supper. Go wash up. I'll start them. Now."

He slipped out of the kitchen and down toward the bathroom. It was clear now — he was getting a last meal. He had never heard of the government working this way, but then he wouldn't have figured that they were going to store government supplies in a shed out in the country, either. Well, they had him. He would wash up, even put on a clean tee shirt. His last meal might as well be kind of nice.

"And Mr. Grundy," she called to him from the kitchen. "He said you could come get your money tomorrow?"

"Mr. Grundy?"

"Yes, I said he was looking for you. He waited a while."

Grundy? That's who was looking for me? That it wasn't the G-men looking for him settled on him slowly but, eventually, it made sense. It had been hours since Tommy found Butch, Butch found Sandy, and they had gone to warn Sluggo at the slaughterhouse behind the butcher shop. In a town the size of Tierra, Hoskins could have taken the government men to their houses or anywhere else in five minutes. They weren't looking for the boys, at least not yet. He would not have to tell his mother anything. At least not yet.

Nor would any of the boys have had to explain anything if Shirley had not found the carton of Lucky Strikes in Butch's room.

"So, of course I know the wetbacks. Have to go out there all the time."

Hoskins was utterly perplexed why the feds were asking him about the Mexicans. He had seen them park the government car in front of the courthouse. There was nothing unusual about that; it's where they usually parked when they were going up to the ration clerk's desk on the second floor or across the street to scare that chicken Fleming, at the bank. He had taken the precaution of calling Reilly on the telephone to tell him that "there were too many olives in the groceries, and the meat wasn't very good either." That had been the standard signal anytime the government car stopped in town. Reilly had said he would "get rid of the bad meat." A few minutes later the jailer had come in to say that two guys from the FBI were in the outer office. Hoskins told him to take them up to the second floor where the ration office was. When the jailer said no, they wanted to see him, he thought they were in the wrong town, a suspicion that dwindled when they walked in, closed the door, and asked the sheriff if he ever went out to the labor camp where the field workers lived.

"Sure. The usual. Jose gets drunk, Jose B waves a knife around. Usual Saturday night stuff with the wetbacks. Nothin' special. Won't even be that for long — you men seen the cotton? Biggest cotton anyone ever seen around here. Say they'll get 200 pounds an acre if the boll weevils are down. That'll take the firewater and switchblades out of 'em." Hoskins wanted them to know the cotton crop was fine this year, in case they were connected to the government buyers who would come for the cotton crops in a few months.

"Did you investigate a rape out there about a month ago?"

"No, can't say I did."

"Do you know anything about a girl — what's her name, Randall?"

"Hinojosa," Agent Randall said after glancing through a file folder.

"Do you know anything about a girl named Hinojosa getting raped, Sheriff?"

"First I heard of it."

"Report says she was picked up and taken to Clovis, raped, left off on the side of the road."

"Naw, never heard nothing about it. 'Sides, if there was, the *padrones* out there'd just make her marry the guy and that'd be the end of it. Happens all the time. This one of them Mann Act things?"

"A Mann Act thing?"

"Yeah, takin' a girl across the state line for immoral purposes. Ain't that the Mann Act? Why else would you federal men be after a girl out at the labor camp?"

"We're not at liberty to tell you."

"Fine by me. Well, don't know nothing about it. You been out there?"

"We can't tell you that, either. But we want to be sure you are telling us in our official investigation that you didn't have any contact with the family of, what's her first name?"

"Guadalupe."

"Guadalupe Hinojosa about a sex assault on the girl, about a month ago, when someone took her in a car from Tierra to the State Line Bar in Clovis? You didn't go out to the labor camp and investigate that, is that what you are saying?"

"Don't know nothing about it. Sorry couldn't help. Only times I go out there is to pick up a drunk or stop a knife fight, somethin' like that."

"All right. Next question, Sheriff. Do you know a federal employee, the post master here, Mr. Bart Sullivan?"

Back inside their green sedan, the government men wrote in their report that Sheriff Hoskins had been cooperative. "But, when asked about the postmaster, these agents believe Sheriff Hoskins was not being forthright, especially when asked if anyone had ever referred to him as *el cartero*."

For his part, after the government men closed their snappy file folder and went out and went back to their olive green sedan, Hoskins thought about going to the *Times* to tell Poppy. *Damn, he'll want to know why I didn't call him first.* He decided that he didn't need Poppy griping at him. He also thought about going over to the post office, but if the G-men were watching him, or even if they later heard that he was warning Bart, it would look bad for him. Unable to come up with a better answer after the men had left than while they had been there, Hoskins' final response was the same one he muttered when they had first asked him if he knew Bart Sullivan, and which Reilly, too, had said when Hoskins had warned him to get rid of all black market meat and hide the fake ration coupons.

"Uh oh."

Hoyt knocked on the barber shop door, then the window, but it was clear that Bradley wasn't open. He walked back over to grocery store and asked if they knew where Mr. Bradley was, but Mr. Reilly, and even Mrs. Reilly, were busy in the back of the store and hadn't seen him. It was near quitting time anyway, so he thought maybe Old Bradley had gone to the drug store. Mr. Bradley was not there, either, nor was he at Nona's having coffee.

"No, fact is he hasn't been around in a few days, Hoyt. Sure is good to have you home. Can I get you a piece of pie? On me?"

"Naw, thanks, but maybe later."

He found Bradley at home.

"What do you want?"

"It's, me, Mr. Bradley. Hoyt."

"I know who you are. What do you want?" Bradley stood inside the screen door and kept Hoyt outside, on the porch.

"I come to town just to see you, Mr. Bradley."

"When you got around to it."

No one had walked over to Bradley's house to tell him that Hoyt Carter had gotten off the bus, not that Sunday when it happened, nor the next day either because the barber shop was closed on Monday. The first Bradley knew that his son's army buddy was alive, was not in a Japanese prisoner of war camp nor even in the Pacific, but was at home four miles outside of Tierra, was Wednesday, when Sandy came by to sweep the barber shop and asked him if it wasn't great, about Hoyt being home and all. Sandy hadn't expected Old Bradley to fly off the handle. Mr. James, who ran the abstract office next door to the *Times*, had been in the barber chair at the time; he was even more thoughtless than Sandy.

"Sure is. Haven't you heard? Hoyt got away and the Army brought him home. What are the odds?"

The more he had clipped on James' hair, and the more Sandy had swept and cleaned, the more Bradley knew that no one in the whole damned town, not even Hoyt, cared about Johnny, not enough to come tell him. He had splashed barber water on James' neck, skipped the styptic pencil treatment for the two or three minor cuts he had inflicted on the back of his head, whipped off the drape, and rushed him out of the barber shop with hair clippings all over his shirt and forehead.

"Go home, Sandy."

"But it's…"

"Get out."

Sandy knew something had gone haywire, even if he didn't know what. He watched Bradley lock up and storm away. Bradley had not been seen for the next week.

"I sure am sorry, Mr. Bradley. My folks just took me home and I ain't been to town since. And you don't have a telephone."

Bradley just glared at him through the screen but, when he didn't answer, Hoyt continued.

"I was gonna come on Sunday when we was in town for church, but Ma just wanted us to stay home and be together so we didn't come. And I had to help out the last two days gettin' our old spring harrow and tractor hooked up and ready for sweepin'. So this morning I just told Pa I had to come talk to you, I couldn't put if off any more." He waited to see if Bradley was going to answer but Bradley said nothing; he just stood at the screen and glared at Hoyt.

Hoyt was as uncomfortable looking at Old Bradley as the barber was to see him. He had expected Johnny's father to still look like the man he was the last time they were home on leave, almost a year before Pearl Harbor. He remembered Bradley as a lot like Johnny, short, thin, full of gab, a man who knew everyone and had a story about them. He used to tell everybody who came in for a haircut the score of every football game Johnny and Will and Hoyt and the boys had played in since they were pee wees. He remembered every touchdown, even the passes they caught and Hoyt's missed blocks and Will's failed tackles, and laughed at every one of them. This Bradley, however, wasn't thin — he was skinny, his collar bones sticking out against his thin shirt, his hair blowing over his forehead. This Bradley hadn't shaved in days and his pants weren't buttoned. He didn't have shoes on.

"And I didn't know what to say to you. I been tryin' to know what to say ever since they said I was gonna be sent home. I'm not very good with words, Mr. Bradley, but if it was my dad, I'd want Johnny to tell him. So he would know."

Bradley still didn't answer him, but he opened the screen door and stepped to one side so that Hoyt could come in. He stood there, inside the door, and sized up the man who had grown up with his boy, and the anger mounted. Bradley knew that if he said anything to Hoyt he would lose his temper, yell at him, blame him for being home, and he knew that if he had any more to drink he would be too drunk to hear what happened to Johnny. Instead, he pointed at the one upholstered chair, next to the radio, and meant for Hoyt to sit in it.

"Oh, no sir, you go ahead and sit down. I don't want it."

"Not gonna stay that long?" Bradley couldn't help himself, but he didn't know if he wanted Hoyt to stay long.

"Whatever you want Mr. Bradley. I don't want to be in your way. I'll come back if you want."

"No, just sit down."

"Can I just sit here?" Without waiting for Mr. Bradley to reply he dropped cross legged to the floor. "I'm pretty used to sitting like this."

Bradley eyed him, curious, but then stepped around him and took the upholstered chair for himself, sat, waited.

"So, what are you going to tell me?"

Hoyt waited, trying to come up with words to start. He wasn't very used to talking anyway, and when he began to say a word he had to stop, take in his breath, stop, and begin again.

"Cat got your tongue?"

"Sorry, Mr. Bradley. Listen. I'm sorry. I'm real sorry. There wasn't anything I could do."

"What happened? How'd you get out and him left behind?"

"Left behind?"

"Yeah. How'd you get out of the POW camp? Why didn't you get out together?"

That was the one thing Hoyt had not heard or even considered — that Mr. Bradley believed they were in a POW camp. He started to ask where Mr. Bradley had gotten that idea, then realized it had been over two years since the Japanese had overrun them on the Bataan Peninsula. Neither Hoyt nor Johnny had ever been in a Japanese POW camp; two years went by before Hoyt had been taken off Mindoro Island in a submarine. He caught his breath, then made a decision.

"Those camps, Mr. Bradley, they're not right. What did you hear about the Philippines?"

Mr. Bradley said only that he knew the Japs had been cruel the way they marched the boys away at Bataan, what he read in the papers. "It was Poppy who got it from the Red Cross, that you was in a camp."

"Well, the camp was pretty rough, Sir. It was two days march and a lot of boys didn't make it to camp."

"But Johnny? He made it, and you made it."

"Yes, Sir," Hoyt lied. He didn't feel good about lying, but it didn't take a doctor to see that Old Bradley would feel worse about the truth. "Yes,

Sir, but we was sick. Everybody was. And then when they started the transports…"

"What's that?"

"They was taking us and putting us on ships to go off to Japan. For slave labor."

"So, he's in Japan? Is that what it is? They took him off to be a slave? Oh, God, my boy."

Hoyt thought about lying again but he knew Johnny wasn't coming home.

"No, Sir. I wish it was, but no, Sir. The Japs just took the ones who wasn't so sick, and Johnny, well…"

Bradley began to cry. He knew that Hoyt had come to tell him that Johnny was dead; it had just been a matter of hearing how.

"We all was sick, Sir. There hadn't been anything we could do, long before we surrendered. You get sick there, real sick."

That much was true. Malaria had come quickly, followed by dysentery. When they surrendered, the Japanese had separated the soldiers who looked too sick to march from Bataan to Camp O'Donnell or Cabanatuan. They were taken away from the others.

"He just drifted off, Sir. I don't think he knew. He just didn't make it."

Bradley sat there, crying, for a long time. He put his hands on his knees, rocked back and forth on the upholstered chair, closed his eyes, opened them, stopped breathing for some time. He finally took in enough breath to stay alive, then thanked Hoyt for telling him.

"Thank you Hoyt. I'm sorry I was hard on you."

"It's all right, Mr. Bradley." Bradley was not nearly as hard on Hoyt as Hoyt was on himself.

"And you, Hoyt. Are you all right?"

"Yes, Sir. I'm all right."

"You look all right, Hoyt. Yes, you look all right. Did they rescue you?"

"Sort of, yes, Sir."

"All of you, is that what happened?"

"No Sir, just three or four of us."

"Well, good, Hoyt. Good. I'm glad you got rescued."

"I wish it had been Johnny, Sir. I was with him every day, from the day we signed up right up until, well, you know. We did everything together, like we used to do, on the team. Just like that, Sir."

"I know you did, Hoyt, I know. And Johnny's probably glad that you got away and he's smilin' down on you right now."

"Yes, sir."

Bradley cried for another minute, not as loudly, then tried to compose himself so that he would not lose touch with Hoyt.

"Hoyt, why'd you boys run off anyway?"

"What do you mean?"

"To join the army? Why'd you run off? You havin' your folks' farm to work, and Shirley Fleming there and all? I thought you two was crazy to join up, but Johnny said you was like the Three Musketeers, you and Will and Johnny. Guess you know all about Will, don't you?"

"My dad told me he's probably in France in the medical corps. Sure glad he wasn't with us that time. But that's about it."

"Well, you know he and Virginia Sullivan eloped right before he shipped out, and now she's gonna have a baby any day now."

"Virginia. Yes, Sir. I haven't seen her either, not yet. But that's great. And a baby, well…"

"You boys should have gone off to college like Will."

There was no reason for Bradley to say this other than as the barber it was in his nature to say whatever was politic to keep a conversation going. Johnny Bradley was no more destined for college than he was to be President. Hoyt had never considered anything except staying at home and living on the family farm. Bradley knew these facts as well as Hoyt did.

"Well, the truth is there wasn't a future here, not for us. When you're a kid you don't know anything but if we had ever known how to say it, we'd have said we joined up because there wasn't no future here. Only room for one barber, so what was Johnny gonna do? And me? My folks' place barely supports them, and with Jim Ned and Nell growin' up, I was just going to be an extra mouth for them to feed. But we didn't know how to say that so what we said was "Here's a buck for a quart," and that's how we wound up joinin' the Army."

"Never heard that one. What's it mean, 'here's a buck for a quart?'"

"Mean? It means here's a dollar and give me a quart jar of that peach brandy or whatever Bart Sullivan was selling." Hoyt hadn't thought about that for a long time, and the memory made him laugh in a reminiscent, bittersweet sort of way.

"Bart was selling jug liquor for a dollar?"

"Of course he was. He always did, ever since he was in high school. That's where we always got our hooch. Bet Johnny'd laugh out loud if he heard us talkin' about buying a quart of white lightning from Bart Sullivan. Between you and me, Johnny and I always thought he was a real turd."

"He is a turd. Guess you know Poppy got him fixed up as postmaster to keep him out of the draft."

"Not surprised."

"Yep. One day Mr. Mason announced he was retiring and leaving town and the next day they made Bart Sullivan to be the postmaster. First job he ever had in his life. Convenient, too, right before he was about to get drafted."

"Wasn't his only job. He made a mean hooch. And he worked for Poppy in the paper some, mixing up ink and setting it up. I remember him telling us that's how he learned to make brandy out of sugar and juice, all the stuff he had to learn how to do at the paper. Makes you laugh, don't it."

"He wasn't going to get drafted anyway. Doc Pritchard had already given him flat feet and high blood pressure and piles and shingles and one-eyed blindness, whatever it took to keep out of the draft. But Poppy wanted insurance, and what better than a government job."

"So now Bart's like his dad. Knows every piece of mail everybody sends and gets."

"And reads it, too. Puts Virginia's letters on the post office wall for everybody to read anytime he's mad at her. I won't even go there any more." He didn't mention that Mrs. Tarlton had the key to his mail box and Sandy brought him his mail. It wasn't important. "So, what'd that have to do with the army? His hooch?"

"He used to sell us a jar after the football games. We'd all scrounge up nickels and pennies and meet him out on the Cemetery Road after a dance or late at night and he'd give us a bottle and we'd pay him. But he came up real mad at us there at the end. We didn't think anything of it, but he showed up at the graduation dance even though he was out two years. And he was trying to dance with Shirley Fleming. Well, I was too, but Shirley wasn't having any of it. She was still trying to catch Will and Will was always stuck on Virginia, but any time Bart would ask her she'd tell him no, and he probably saw me trying to dance with her, too. Then he was tryin' to dance with Molly, and she never ever danced with anybody but Johnny, never. Whatever happened to Molly, anyway?"

"Molly? She run off. Right after you boys…" Mr. Bradley didn't finish his thought. "Molly left home after Johnny and Hoyt were reported captured in Bataan. Her parents called everybody to ask if she was there, and she wasn't. They checked with Arnie to see if she had got on the train and with Homer to see if she had got on the bus. Hoskins had no idea where she was. A month later she wrote to say she was working in a munitions factory in San Angelo and not coming home until Johnny came home."

"Well, Bart was probably drinking his own liquor and not holding it but we said we needed to buy a jar, and he told us to meet him except to go out on the road to the quarry, not on Cemetery Road. We didn't think nothing of it and we went out there and waited and waited. Finally about midnight Will gave up and went home, but Johnny and I was just two bumpkins on a pumpkin, in the dark, waiting for Bart. Well, Bart showed up and he said "Hi fellers. Sorry I'm late and here's the hooch." So we gave him a dollar and he said he had two jars and just take the other one, so we'd each have one. And we said thanks and would he like a drink himself and he said he had to be going. We asked for a ride back to town but he said no, if we spilt anything in Poppy's coupe there'd be hell. Well, he wasn't gone five minutes and us walking down that road and Hoskins showed up. Didn't Johnny tell you this?"

"He never told me a thing. What happened?"

"Hoskins pulled up in that damned old truck and said 'Stop! Right there!' And he got out and he knew damned good and well Bart had sold us that brandy. And he said, 'You boys is under arrest for minors in possession and drinking in a dry county.' Anyway, by the time he had us in the jail, he said we was gonna get six months and what did we know? Then he said he had been knowing our folks a long time and it was gonna be hard on you seeing us go off to jail, and being criminals, and we'd never get a job with jail on our records. Well, by morning, we were begging to go to the army if he'd let us off, and he practically drove us to Lubbock to sign the papers. We were just stupid kids."

Bradley didn't say anything, didn't know what to say. He sat in the upholstered chair, rocking back and forth, staring off into space. Hoyt waited as well; he had learned to sit and wait for hours at a time without moving and without being seen. To be sitting on the floor of a real house, in front of Mr. Bradley, held no danger. After what may have been a half hour, the roar of airplane engines interrupted them. Mr. Bradley twitched enough to show Hoyt that he was conscious again, aware that he was in his home with his son's buddy on the floor in front of him, and that he should do something. The engines drew near and he stood up. Hoyt stood up as well. He could see that Mr. Bradley had begun to cry, not loud or embarrassingly, but with tears rolling down his face and dropping onto his shirt.

"I'm sorry I had to come home and tell you all this, Sir."

"No, Hoyt, you did the right thing. Thanks."

"I wish it was me there, and Johnny was here. I know that's easy to say, but it's true."

"It's all right Hoyt. I knew Johnny was dead. You just have a feeling, and I had it. I shouldn't have let Poppy convince me otherwise. But I thought you was dead too, so what do I know." Bradley's tears continued to flow but he stood up straight and faced Hoyt, then took his hand and shook it, like a man. Without quite knowing how he managed to walk Hoyt past the screen door and out on to the porch.

"I can come back, Sir," Hoyt volunteered. He noticed the porch, loose boards, a pile of chicken wire, rotted garden hoses under the front window. The grass was dead. The flower beds were barren. "Do you need some help around the place? I'll be glad to do it. Fact is my little brother, and my sister too, they do everything out at the place, and Pa acts like I shouldn't be helping out with the chores."

"Sure, Hoyt. You come on back. It's good to see you, and I thank you for coming." He shook Hoyt's hand again and waited, watching the soldier walk out to the street, turn, wave, and walk away toward town. Bradley waved back, absently, a reflex, but his mind still dwelled on the history of Johnny being tricked into joining the army.

He didn't know everything, but he knew some things, and Mr. Bradley decided he had had enough of Bart Sullivan and Sheriff Hoskins.

The airplanes flew directly east, from the west, out of the sun, and began to descend from five thousand feet. About two miles from Tierra they leveled off at two hundred feet above ground and turned to aim directly at the water tower. The pilots made the slight adjustment to fly single file and, just before they would have hit the water tower, they climbed, opened their bomb bays, and screamed over the town, then turned south toward the cemetery.

"I am so tired of those airplanes," Virginia shouted as she walked in the front door. "It seems like every day there are more of them, and they get so close."

Poppy looked up from the composition table, saw his daughter more than heard her, and looked to make sure the trash basket where the news wire sheets fell was still empty. It was.

"They make the air pound, vibrating, it's a wonder the enemy doesn't just run away from being scared to death. Mrs. Reilly says the milk tastes so bad because they scare the cows. Is there any news, Poppy?"

"No, nothing special. Ike gave Patton another command. In France."

"Who's Patton?"

"Only general we have with real guts," he answered. "Ike fired him in Sicily after he took the whole island. Embarrassed the British so Ike had to fire him to keep our allies happy. Now they gave him another army and sent him to France."

This information about France was not sufficiently specific to peak Virginia's interest. She sorted through the news wires. MacArthur was getting closer to the Philippines. Cotton Ed Smith lost in the South Carolina senate race. A mixture of onion and garlic paste reportedly improves circulation ('people who eat it are given more breathing room ....'). Cuba was close to a military dictatorship. Poppy had already burned the story of the newspaper photographer who was killed in St. Lô after the battle was over when an American bomb fell short.

"Will may be in his unit," Poppy went on. "No way to know until you hear from him. But he better put on his running shoes if Patton gets turned loose. He'll be in Berlin in a month."

She finished leafing through the wires, then sat heavily in Poppy's wooden desk chair, her abdomen bulging almost up to her chest.

"Then we won't learn anything until your little felon delivers my mail. These practice bombings are going to do what Doc can't. This baby kicks like mad every time they come over."

Even Poppy could not turn a blind eye to the sentiment, his grandchild pushing and kicking and trying to get started in the world. He put the lead plates down and took off his heavy apron, then went over to sit by Virginia and admire her belly.

"Gonna be here any day."

"It'd be nice to hear from his father," she replied.

"He's all right, Dear. If anything had happened I'd get it off the wire. If you weren't here waiting to get it yourself."

"I meant to hear from him, not about him. I haven't gotten a letter, not in my hands anyway, in months. Bart has them and you know it, Poppy."

It was getting harder to take Bart's side. He had quietly built up more than just a grip on people. It would be nearly impossible to trace it through the bank books or find the deeds and contracts, but Poppy had put plenty aside, first for Bart and now for that grandbaby, all by his creed of 'taking the long view.' He had told Bart a hundred times to take the long view but the boy had a streak in him that Poppy had not been able to train out of him. When Bart did a thing, he did it until he was tired of it, not until it was smart to stop.

"Oh, don't believe that, Gin."

"It's true. Bart hasn't given me a single letter...not even on the bulletin board...since...."

Since Bart had been afflicted with the single worst case of the runs Doc had ever seen. That had started three or four days after Bart had eaten half of a chocolate cake. Poppy had figured it out.

"What's for dinner tonight?"

"How about a steak?"

"You're kidding."

"Nope, Reilly was giving them away."

"Not like Reilly to give anything away."

"I was there an hour ago and there was a line from the cash register to the back wall. Everybody got something — steaks, roast, pork chops, and thick ones, too. He gave me six T-bones, two for each of us. There was an accident over at the butcher shop and he had to get rid of them."

Poppy knew what that meant — Reilly had gotten scared, probably of government inspectors finding all the black market meat in his locker, and was trying to get the town to eat all the evidence in his grocery store. *He should have called me — him or Hoskins!* It was suspicious but unlikely that Virginia knew anything about it. He thought about mentioning in a casual way his observation that there seemed to have been a surge of "extra" ration stamps. She probably knew better than anyone who the traders were because she steadfastly refused to "borrow" any that Poppy or Bart had heard were up to swap, just like she had refused to steal any when she was the ration clerk. *All righty,* he decided. *If no one wants to let me know what's going on, I'll let Hoskins and Reilly worry about it themselves for a change.*

"Your mother used to cook steaks for me, do you remember?"

"Mother?" The sudden change in his voice surprised her.

"Oh, yes. She had this way of using two skillets. She'd put the burner under one, get it real hot, put a steak in it for just a second or two and kind of burn it, then flip it over and burn the other side, and then take it off and put it in the other skillet over real low heat and let it just sort of cook in there, slow. When it was ready to eat she'd drop it back in the hot skillet and seal it all up and make it black."

Virginia was caught off-guard. Poppy, always angry with her, never talked about Emma. She believed that he blamed her for his wife having faded away. Several months after they put her in the state asylum Virginia had become the head cheerleader; he had refused to go to the football games. He stayed away from the homecoming dance, the graduation dance, and would probably have not gone to her high school graduation if he could have come up with a good enough excuse. Since then he had only driven with her to Lubbock once or twice, in the car, to see her mother, and when they drove he refused to talk to Virginia. He even had told her that he planned to eat Thanksgiving dinner at Nona's Café because he didn't want to watch Virginia wreck a good turkey and greens just because Will Hastings was home on leave. In fact, the only times she could remember him seeming interested in her at all was when the ration office opened and, now, after she had turned up pregnant. Even those moments were short-lived; as soon as she adjusted Poppy had resumed his general indifference.

"We didn't have it very often. There wasn't a lot of steak then because there wasn't any cattle or any money either. Ranchers watched their herds die off in the Depression and we didn't have two nickels to rub together. But we were all right, Virginia. We had enough and we took care of you. And Bart too. We were all right."

She was amazed; he was smiling, tender even, if that was what it was like to be tender.

"I'm sorry, Poppy. I do wish I knew how to be like Mother. I know I'm not turning out very good."

"Don't be sorry. It'd be nice if she was here for you, especially when Little Will comes. She'd like that, a lot. She could sew things up for him like she did for you. I don't think you had any store bought clothes, not until you were ten or eleven. I'd come home and your mother would be sitting at that machine, treadle humming, sewing away. And you and Shirley would sit there on the floor and get the scraps to make dolls. Whatever happened to your rag dolls? Do you remember your rag dolls?"

"Miss Willifer."

"Miss Willifer."

"She's in my closet."

"Shame you don't see Shirley any more. Guess people grow up. She's kind of a snob, isn't she, now that she's a teacher?"

Virginia wondered how her father could know all there was to know, facts about Mussolini and cotton prices and where rubber came from, and everything in Tierra too, who had tires and who had extra ration stamps and how to find a job for Sandy's father and the other men after the cotton gin burned down, and not know about the fight between his own daughter and her ex-friend.

"We used to laugh, your mother and I, before she got sick. Poor old Fleming, afraid of his own shadow. And his kids turned out to think they were better than anybody else in town. It's a good thing Will picked you,

Virginia. Shirley would have made him pay to be married to her, the banker's daughter. She would have made him pay."

"What else did Mother do, Poppy?"

"Oh, I don't know. She just took care of us. Really took care of us. I miss her, Virginia." He steadied himself, put a hand on the table and hoped that Virginia didn't notice.

"I miss her too, Poppy. I'm sorry she's sick."

"Me too, Dear. Me too. Tell you what, let's lock up and go home and you cook us up a couple of steaks. I'll come back later and finish the paste-up. If we can get the paper out early tomorrow, we'll take Thursday off and go to Lubbock."

"We don't have to do that, Poppy. Go to Lubbock."

"No, we need to go. You need some things for Little Will. Let's go get them. Diapers and bottles and all that. Think you can keep him in there a couple of more days?"

Knowing that it was more likely that she would 'keep him in there' a couple of weeks instead of a couple of days, she answered that she could hold him off long enough to go to Lubbock with GrandPoppy. This made him smile, and he hugged her.

"You have her mouth, you know. People say you take after me and Bart takes after her, but you've got her mouth."

Virginia had never believed that she looked like Emma Sullivan in any way. No one who saw her thick auburn hair would have thought of them as mother and daughter. She involuntarily touched her lips with her forefinger, grazed it along the contours of her mouth, and lightly licked her tongue over the surfaces.

"Not her mouth, mouth. Her words. She could pop off faster than Will Rogers, kept me laughing all the time. Oh, she was good to look at, just like you, but it was what she said that I loved about your mother." Poppy didn't say it but it was because Virginia was so quick with words, a joke, a smart remark, that every time she spoke he heard Emma and missed her. It wasn't fair to Virginia, he knew that, to avoid her because she reminded him of Emma, but he couldn't help it.

I'll do better, he said to himself. *I've got to do better, and I will.* He should have said it to Virginia, but there were limits. They walked out of the *Times*. He turned off the lights, closed the door, and ignored the wire printer as it began to spit the next dispatch of news from France.

Virginia would always remember the night she had cooked a steak for Poppy. She forgot the details, the promise to go to Lubbock and the concern about the well-being of Miss Willifer, but she never forgot the night she tried to use two skillets to cook his steak, just like he wanted. It was the nearest she and Poppy ever got to affection before he disappeared.

"All right. See that cemetery? That's your IP. What's your range and bearing when you cross the cemetery? A mile at one-sixty-five magnetic. When we cross the cemetery you've got it."

The student bombardier clicked his microphone, acknowledged the instructor, and peered into the Norden bombsight. The cemetery came into view immediately below them. The pilot began to turn south, to one hundred-sixty-five degrees, and at the same moment, like a quarterback taking the ball from the center, the bombardier said "I've got it." He peered into the bombsight, made a slight adjustment, the aircraft yawed very slightly to the left, and straightened. Almost immediately a row of elm trees came into view at the top of the bomb sight.

"Aiming point?" the instructor asked.

"Pond, then shed."

"The shed is a ball bearing factor…" but before the instructor could finish, the student bombardier finished the exercise.

"Away! Away! Away!" he shouted into the microphone. Immediately the four engines roared, the propellers straining at the load. The heavy airplane banked hard and climbed as the bomb bay doors closed and the target area disappeared behind them.

"Good job. Good job," the instructor shouted over the roaring engines. Another instructor, squatting in the cockpit between the two pilots in training, complimented their precision response to the bomb drop and decided that he would not make them do another practice run. A third instructor began to grade the navigator.

"Okay, listen up. That was it. I graded you out at ninety-one percent. If the other crews," he said, waving his hands toward the rear to refer to the other training bombers who were still finishing their runs, "if the other crews grade out, we'll start tomorrow on the dummies."

The dummies were hollow bomb casings, the same size as an armed bomb, and loaded with sand to the proper weight.

"And in about a week we'll see if you guys can knock that shed down. Beer's on me."

The headsets rang with cheers as the B-24 climbed to eight thousand feet and headed toward Clovis. Every man on the plane felt ready and, despite the certainty that graduation day meant shipping out to Europe or the Pacific, the team had no doubt that they could destroy the ball bearing factory on the first try.

CHAPTER ELEVEN

August 30, 1944

"Ask her. She'll know." Agent Randall laughed. "If anyone'll know it's her. Looks like she could pop at any time." He pulled the sedan over to the side of the street and rolled down his window.

"Excuse me, Ma'am. Could you tell us where Dr. Pritchard's office is?"

Virginia looked at the driver, then at his passenger. Despite the scorching heat, both men wore suits, their neckties drooping, the agents having driven seventy miles with the windows down. Their hats were little help against the fierce sun. She was tempted to say no but didn't.

"Two blocks north and you'll come to the square. Turn left. Two blocks more, turn the corner, it's on your right." She pointed in the direction of the courthouse, then turned her hand to point west to be clear which way to turn.

"Thanks," the driver replied, touching the brim of his hat. He engaged the clutch, shifted into first, and eased away so as to not kick dust onto the pregnant lady.

For her part, for no reason she could think of, she stood to watch the car as it eased toward the center of Tierra, then waved as it drove away from her.

Mrs. Tarlton watched from her perch inside Nona's, but didn't say anything to anyone at the moment. She had to think about what it might mean. After all, one government car had already come to town that day. She had seen it when she went to get her mail.

"Bart, take your shirt off and have a seat up here on the table."

Bart looked at the two men, then at Doc Pritchard, then back at them.

They had come into the post office around six. He had heard the door open but he was in the back room sorting through the day's private letters and couldn't see out front. After a few moments it had occurred to him, not consciously but at some lower level, that it was too quiet. Whoever had come in should have opened their post office box, taken out the mail, closed the box door. Or walked around to the bulletin board. Or left the post office. He looked up. Two men were inside the back room, standing behind him.

"Bart Sullivan?" one of them had asked.

"Who are you?"

They had taken out some kind of badge. He should have looked at it but the sight of it scared him so badly that he not only didn't read the badge, he didn't hear what they said when they told him who they were. He only heard the word "agency."

"Come with us, Bart. Just leave the mail there. But let's turn off the lights."

One of the men reached out and took Bart by the arm, not roughly, but in a way that let him know he was not free to decline. The other man took the mail from him, laid it on the counter top, and patted it into a tidy square pile. They seemed to know the layout of the post office, he reflected. "Let's lock the door, here," one of them had said. The agent then had taken his keys and locked up the office area, leaving the front door open for anyone who might come in later to check their mail boxes. Then they turned him around, switched off the office lights, and walked Bart out through the back door. They paused a moment while the agent fumbled with the keys to find the one and lock it as well.

"Where are we going? What do you want?"

They didn't answer but when they arrived at Doc Pritchard's office there was another man waiting inside the front door.

"How ya' feeling today, Bart Sullivan?" one of them asked. "Stomach ache? Maybe a little fever? You seem to be sweating?" They laughed, not like laughing at a joke, more like a snicker. The man who was already in Doc Pritchard's office said nothing, just walked behind them to stand between Bart and the door. Bart thought he had seen the man somewhere before, a remotely familiar face, but he couldn't quite place him.

The door that led back to the examining rooms opened and Doc Pritchard emerged, escorted by yet another agent. Doc looked shaken. His hair was unkempt and his face was even redder than usual. He and Bart exchanged glances. Randall's report would reflect that "the look on Doctor Pritchard's face was, in my opinion, an attempt to communicate to the subject that Doctor Pritchard was not able to warn him or help him and the look on the subject's face was that he did not know what was happening and he was apprehensive."

Together they all walked back to the examining room.

"Bart Sullivan, have a seat there. Take your shirt off," Agent Lambert instructed him. He didn't look like a doctor but, then Bart didn't have the gumption to refuse. He took his shirt off, then his undershirt. "That's good. Here, take a look at this."

He handed Bart a document, a stiff paper form printed on brown government stock paper.

"Is that your signature there, Bart Sullivan?" He pointed to an ink signature on the bottom of the form.

It was.

"Doctor Pritchard, is that Mr. Sullivan's signature? Right there next to your signature?"

Doc Pritchard looked more than shaken. He was scared. Bart peered across the form as the man held it out for him to see, hoping there was a mistake, as if by some remote chance someone had forged their names. "Report of Medical Examination" it said across the top. "Examiner's statement of medical condition for Armed Forces."

"Doctor Pritchard, according to this form, it looks like Mr. Sullivan here wasn't doing too well when you examined him for military conscription. The draft. Let's see. He has flat feet. You looked at his feet and you found that they were flat feet, isn't that right, Doctor?"

Pritchard looked away.

"And blood pressure. You took his blood pressure, I see. My heavens, this boy must have been on the edge of fainting. How bad is 175 over 145? I don't get those numbers, but they sure sound like high blood pressure to me. Is that right, Doctor Pritchard? Is that what Bart Sullivan's blood pressure was back when you saw him on, when was this? February 1942? Right after Pearl Harbor, that's right. High blood pressure after Pearl Harbor."

Pritchard didn't answer but everyone in the room could see that he was shaking so badly that he might not be able to talk. He wanted a drink.

"And look at this. This young man has a heart murmur. He could not possibly do basic military training with a heart murmur. No climbing over barricades for a man with a heart murmur. No carrying a rifle for a man with high blood pressure. Is that right, Doctor? And march? Forget it. How could a man in this shape march with those flat feet?"

The man who had been waiting in Doc's office withdrew a form. "Clovis General Hospital."

"This here's Doctor Martinez, over from Clovis. Do you remember meeting him, Bart Sullivan?"

And then Bart remembered. Seeping through his fear of these men was a hazy memory of the night he had gotten into a fight. A cop had taken him over to the hospital where this Mexican had poked around on him and cleaned him up. Hoskins had followed him back to Tierra.

Bart Sullivan knew his run was over.

"Can I talk to my father?"

"Your father?"

"Yes, could I talk to my father. He can tell me…"

"Bart Sullivan, this is a Selective Service physical. For the draft. Do you understand that? We are a special board of the United States Armed Forces Selective Service Agency. It has come to our attention that a young man named Bart Sullivan, age 26, of Tierra, Texas, was examined by a Doctor Martinez, who happens to be with us, in Clovis New Mexico, and found to be — do I get this right, Doctor Martinez? — found to be of age for military service and with no apparent disqualifying medical conditions, except for a cut lip and a black eye. So, this special board has convened here in the Tierra medical examiner's office and brought you here for a medical examination to determine your fitness for the armed services. And boys who come to doctors' offices for medical examinations to determine their fitness for the armed services don't have their daddies in the room. Do you understand that?"

He understood. It was out of his hands for the moment but later, when they were through, he would talk to Poppy. Poppy would fix it, because Bart was the postmaster of Tierra. The postmaster is an essential job and he was an essential war worker. In fact, when Poppy finished with these men, they'd be the ones shipped off to the army. *These jokers don't know the connections Poppy Sullivan has.* Bart believed these wild thoughts with all his heart.

Doctor Martinez went around behind the table. He put a stethoscope against Bart's back, then moved it to his chest. He listened, then moved it again and listened again.

"Doctor Pritchard, I find no murmur. Would you like to listen?"

Pritchard took his own stethoscope out and made a perfunctory jab at listening to Bart's chest. When Bart looked up at him, Pritchard shook his head. Dr. Martinez made some entries on a clean brown paper form.

"Let me take your blood pressure here, young man." Dr. Martinez attached a cuff to Bart's arm and began to pump up the pressure. He looked at the vacuum gauge as it fell, then released the pressure, then looked at the gauge again.

"Let's rest a moment and do it again. You may have what we call 'examiner's anxiety.'"

Bart perked up at this news. Maybe he really did have high blood pressure.

"While we do this, let me look at your feet."

There was nothing wrong with his feet, or his eyes, ears, nose, throat, or temperature. His pulse was not a cause for remark.

"Doctor Pritchard, let's do the blood pressure one more time and we're through. Would you like to observe?"

Doctor Martinez wrapped the cuff again, pumped it up again, and watched as the instrument measured the systolic pressure. He wrote it on the form, then watched as the diastolic pressure held and recorded it as well.

"Well, Mr. Sullivan, you definitely have high blood pressure."

Bart couldn't believe his luck.

"I took it twice. Normal should be around 110 or so over 80 or so, a little either side is fine. But yours, well, look at this. You have 118 over 90. Then, second time, 116 over 90. My guess is that you drink too much beer. But that'll be all right, because your blood pressure will go right down as soon as they put you in basic training. As for 175 over 145, well, I have good news Mr. Sullivan. You're not dead. With that blood pressure, you wouldn't have lasted. And when I saw you in Clovis, you had, let me see. Yes, 114 over 85. Gentlemen, I find no disqualifying medical conditions in Mr. Sullivan. I find that this man is fit for induction into the armed forces." He jotted a few notes and made some check marks on the conscription medical form, then signed it and offered it to Doc. Doc looked at it, then turned his head and refused to look at any of them.

Bart looked up. The men looked back. One handed him his shirt.

"You'll need this. Not for long, but for the ride. And put your shoes on too."

"The ride?"

"Yes, the ride. Like I said, we are a special board. We're special enough that we're able to give you a ride. Let's go."

They took Bart out and put him in the back seat of the green sedan. Randall got in behind the wheel and the other agents got in the back seat, one on either side of Bart. The doors closed.

Dr. Martinez knocked on the sedan's window and the agent rolled it down.

"Mr. Sullivan, there's no shame in going into the army or the navy."

Bart tried to ignore him, turning his face to the front and staring out the windshield.

"Do you know a girl named Lupe Hinojosa?"

Bart did not turn, face the doctor, or make any other sign of recognition. This Mexican had tricked him once already.

"There's no shame in going to the army but there is in what you did to that girl. If it was up to me, you'd be going somewhere a lot different than the service. But it's not up to me."

The sedan backed away from the curb, straightened its wheels, and drove away from the dirty little clinic. As it passed the front door of the post office Bart saw Mrs. Tarlton inside, stooped down to get into Mr. Bradley's oversized mail box. She didn't look up. The sedan turned onto the main street and passed the courthouse square. Bart peered down the cross street to the newspaper office, hoping in vain that Poppy would be out front, that he would see what was happening and chase these G-men down. He hoped that Poppy would stop them and take Bart out of the car and straighten these men out — Bart couldn't go off to the draft, because he was essential.

There was no light in the windows of the *Tierra Times*. *Shit — his car ain't there*, Bart remembered. *It's behind the post office — I'm supposed to be heading to the State Line.*

The sedan drove on.

Bart's last view of Tierra came as the agent's car drove up to the highway and turned east toward Lubbock. He looked at the Magnolia Station; Homer was sitting in front staring at the driveway bell, whittling. He glanced at Nona's Café; light eked out the windows, her feeble neon sign bubbling toward the gravel parking lot. He knew, then, that he was lost. It was Friday night. Poppy would have expected that Bart would drive over to the State Line, and Poppy and Virginia would go to Nona's for supper. No one would miss him before tomorrow, maybe not even until Sunday or Monday if, as he feared, they believed that for the first time, Bart Sullivan had finally gotten lucky. He knew that he would not see the town again.

"I saw her talking to them right before Bart disappeared. That's true. I just happened to be sitting down in Nona's and I was having a cup of coffee and I looked out the window and there it was, right in the middle of the street. It stopped and she stood right there and pointed straight at the post office."

"You can't see the post office from there, Lorene."

"She pointed straight downtown, right at the courthouse, then turned her hand to the left like this — " and Mrs. Tarlton demonstrated exactly what Virginia had done in the street." — and pointed again. It was the post office. She was telling them exactly where to go to find that boy."

"The post office isn't hard to find. It's the only one in town and it's a block from the square. They could have found it in two minutes just by driving into town."

"And when the car drove off, well, she waved! Waved at it. Like I would wave to you. I'm telling you, I saw it. She never did like Bart."

"I won't argue with you about that."

"I sure hope Poppy doesn't hear what she did. I hate to think."

A week later Sandy appeared at the front door.

"Sandy, hello. What are you doing? I haven't seen you for ever. Want to come in?"

"Naw. If you need me to do something, sure, but I've got to be getting back to Reilly's. I brought your mail."

Sandy held out a thick knot of letters, tied in a string. All of them had the familiar cross-hatching of Army V-letters. Most appeared to have been opened. When Virginia saw them, she put her hand to her mouth and stumbled, almost falling to the floor. Sandy reached for her arm but she straightened up, then walked backward and sat down, heavily, on the stuffed chair next to the Philco.

"Are you okay? I don't have to go right back. I can stay awhile. Get you something."

Virginia shook her head, no. She took the letters, stared at them dumbly, then removed the string and began to go through them, quickly reading each envelope, then putting it at the bottom of the stack and reading the next one, and the next, looking for something but not finding it.

"Sandy, where did you get these?"

"At the post office. I was over there to get Mr. Bradley's mail and I saw this new man and I said, 'Hey, who are you?' and he said he was the post man and I said, 'Hey, where's Bart?' and he said, 'I'm just the post man.' And then he asked me if I knew who people are here in town and I said I did and he read their names off some mail and when he came to Virginia Sullivan I said 'Yes, but now she's Mrs. Hastings,' and he looked at the letters and said there sure was a lot of them for Virginia Sullivan, and I said I worked for you and I'd be glad to bring them and he gave them to me."

She was breathing heavily, her back at an angle, her hips shifting in search of any comfort. Sandy was both embarrassed and ashamed to look, her heavy pregnancy laying down against her spread-apart legs that stood out against her thin dress. Shifting constantly on the seat, Virginia clutched the letters with her right hand and her abdomen with her left. One by one she stared at a folded sheet, then rejected it and took up the next, and Sandy knew that she had forgotten he was even in the room.

"Uh, I'll be glad to stay, but if you don't need me…"

She didn't even look up. Sandy's last glimpse of Virginia told him that she appeared to have found what she was looking for, or at least had made a choice. She had unfolded the first V-mail letter and began to read it. He left.

9 July Ste Marie du Vire France: Please ignore my last letter. I need to write to you, even if you don't answer, just so I can be in touch with somebody. This isn't the time for me to believe I'm completely alone so I'll wait for that till after the war, if I make it. We've moved about fifteen miles south of the beaches. It doesn't sound like much but it took almost three weeks of fighting for the division to get out of Isigny and down this far. I can't even count the casualties. The field hospital has been put in reserve in an apple barn, about ¹/₄ mile behind a village and a mile behind the battalion CP. Village is a wreck, church steeple down, houses and post office in ruins, probably from our artillery running Germans out of town. Thought I saw Douglas when a crew brought in a stretcher case — my mind is playing games on me, everybody looks the same: muddy uniform, dead eyes, beard, cigarette hanging out. Guy was gone before I could see if it was him. Antsley (yes, Antsley! Small world!) says more waiting. Will write soon. — Will

Virginia read it again. The letter was more than a month old. She didn't remember Ste. Marie from the Atlas but, wherever he was, Will was in France and close enough to the fighting for them to bring wounded soldiers to him. *Who is Antsley? Why would he think I knew him?*

She considered putting the letters in order but the odd way Will had written the dates distracted her. Because of the way the Army compressed them she had to begin reading the letter just to find out when Will wrote it. Then, after she read the first line of a letter she couldn't stop. For the next hour she read the letters her brother had kept from her.

14 July Ste Marie du Vire France: Sorry haven't written. Doing surgery with sound of tanks and big guns, up all night every night. Op'd on a French Resistance who

got wounded by mine in a barn, brought in with French civilian refugees. Rain slowing things down but suspect things are about to get busy up front, am told we just won major battle across river about eight miles away. Going to FH to check on Garth, may cover for him. — Will

11 June Portsmouth: Back in England. Told we are eligible for assignment here in England because of week doing surgery on LST hospital ship. Trying to find where Peter flew in; people say his glider unit was based somewhere south of London. Worried, high casualties, real high. Can you get Stars and Stripes? — Love, Will

She realized that some letters just said 'Will' while others said 'Love, Will.' She read on.

May 15, 1944: Dear Virginia: I finished field hospital medical officer school and get a weekend leave before next assignment, then probably back to division medical office at the 29th until [~~marked out by censor~~]. I'm planning to meet Peter in London as a graduation present to myself. Douglas set it up. Can't wait; I think about him almost as much as I think about you. He's so funny, goes charging in to everything without a care in the world. I wish I was like him; I love him so much. Suspect he has a girl or more likely a string of them — if he had a mustache he'd look like Errol Flynn, and English girls love our pilots, so I hear. Please write; it would help me a lot to hear from you. — Love, Will

15 July Ste. Marie du Vire France: Assistant division medical officer pulled me over and said I had twenty write-ups for surg. procedures. Read them. Mostly from the

week the battalion was trying to get south of Isigny, lot of mines blowing up legs and feet, some avulsion cases and bowels I chose to not exteriorate. One of the cases was a guy on the LST, so Major Halliburton must have plugged my file before they sent him off to the safe war. ADMO says forget it. 16 July sorry didn't finish the letter, was at the line, MG wounds and a lot of burns from tank rounds, the other battalion's commander was killed. ADMO watched two of my surgeries and said 'division was full of....' Am told Carentan is not more than six miles away, across River, think of Peter all the time. — Will

---

June 1, 1944: Dear Virginia: A last letter. Well, I hope not, but we've been put in trucks and brought someplace that isn't London and isn't Division. All I can say is I see boats and water and a lot of soldiers, a lot! and I'm one of them, hard as it is for me to believe. I've been detailed away from the Division Medical Office and my unit for special duty, which in the army is not a reward. So, this may be the last letter for a while, but not the last. (Bad luck to say that). Missed Peter in London. I wrote some orders for Douglas to go up to London with me ('to a special clinic...'). The two of us caught the train but, well, I don't know what went wrong. I'm pretty disappointed. We made it to the Rainbow Club at Piccadilly and waited but no Peter. (There's a whole story about what happened next — can't put it in a letter but it's probably how I wound up on special duty). When I got back to [~~marked out by censor~~], I had to take care of Major Halliburton's injuries. Anyway, I'm writing to say, well, I'm scared. Here's the truth. Anything can happen. I wanted Peter to tell me we were going to meet up and that everything would be okay like he used to do at the orphanage. (Remember me telling you?) Crazy to still want things like that from your big brother, but everything here is, I don't know. Guys always talk about girls or drinking or baseball but the fact is, I just wanted to see my brother. Tell Shirley thanks for the picture (no letter?). No idea when she took it but you look beautiful and Peter looks like, well, like Peter. It's in my butt pack. Pray for us. I want to come home. Say hello to everyone there for me. All my love, Yours, Will

19 July Ste Marie du Vire: We took St. Lô! Antsley and I were the battalion's forward surgery for the last three days and marched into the rubble of the town with the 116th. Our reward? We got fired! 1st Army is sending me off to look for a place for a new evacuation hospital away from the combat area. If I make it back to Tierra ask me about FUBAR — this is it. Shorty says they sent one of my wound cares back to duty. Antsley put the guy back on a cot to keep him from going back into the line! Tomorrow I am headed for bridge at Pont Hebert in an hour and attached to non-com platoon for next week or so. At least it should be quiet that far behind the line. — Will

That was not the last letter in the stack, but it was the last dated. She folded them and tied them with string. There was a quilted box in her dresser where she kept what few miserable treasures she had; the letters joined the photograph Mrs. Fleming had brought and a locket, with a lock of hair, which she had worn briefly. She held out two letters, then took them back to the chair and read them again, over and over, until Poppy walked in.

"Will wrote," she said.

The house was dark. He assumed she was asleep in her room; her voice from the chair gave him something to focus on.

"In fact, he wrote quite a bit."

"Good," Poppy said. He brushed past her to go to the kitchen.

"Wouldn't you like to hear what he wrote?" she called to him. He paused before he got as far as the refrigerator. The very sound of her voice irritated him, and he turned to stare back at her from the doorway.

"Well, did he write and tell us what happened to your brother? Is that in his letters? Huh? Is it?"

"Not *my* brother, no." Her voice had a sharp and hostile edge but Poppy was not interested in what she had to say and less in how she said it.

"Did he write a nice neat love letter and say "Dear Virginia, is it true that you turned your brother in to the feds and they took him away?" I'll bet that isn't in there, is it?"

It had been a week since Bart's disappearance. Poppy had called in a favor here, another there, but no one could tell him where Bart was. The Federal Bureau of Investigation in Lubbock denied having any interest in Bart Sullivan, then or at any other time. No one from the Office of Price Administration seemed to have heard of him either, although Poppy didn't push them to dig too deeply into the name Sullivan.

"Is it true that you told the feds where to find him?"

"I wish I had. I didn't, but I wish I had."

"So it's true you hated him."

"Who says I told the federal agents where to find Bart, and why would I? I told some men in a government car how to find Doc's office. No one asked me about Bart."

Poppy didn't believe her. He had sent Hoskins to look for Bart in Clovis. Hoskins reported back that the barkeep at the State Line couldn't remember him. No one at the army air field kept track of civilians in civilian bars. Not even the Clovis police knew anything about the postmaster from the little town up the road in Texas, nor seemed much interested. Hoskins had gone out to the Mexican labor camp, too. They always knew more than they should. *No está aquí*, he understood. He thought they were lying but it would take a little time to threaten the truth out of them, and he knew how agitated Poppy was. It also occurred to him that Doc Pritchard liked a little white lightning from time to time. Hoskins reported finding Doc at home in his underwear, a bottle of Jack Daniels on the breakfast table.

"You were seen pointing."

She glared at him from the chair, then struggled to lift herself up and walk into the kitchen. He stepped back to let her walk through the doorway and noticed that she had the letters in her hand.

"Let me share one of Will's love letters with you Poppy. It was already opened when I got it, so maybe you and Bart have already read it. Listen to this," she said, and held up one of the V-mails to read aloud.

20 June Isigny France: I should have told you. I told the Army to put Peter's things in a box and ship to me in Tierra in care of you. I don't have anywhere else to send things. If I make it back I'll come to Tierra for it. Thank you — Will

"Well, what do you think of that, Poppy? Today is August 10. Let me see, that's fifty days, more or less. How long do you think it takes to get a box here?"

"I don't know. Why would I know?"

"Arnie says three or four weeks, more or less. Say late July."

"Arnie doesn't know how long it takes the Army to send a box."

"Sure he does. He says it arrived a couple of weeks ago. And he gave it to you. You and the law north of the Pecos."

"I don't know anything about a box, Virginia," he said. His face was the color of old ashes. Poppy turned away.

This time he's really lying, she thought. *He always lies to me, but usually by just not telling me something, or changing the subject. This time he's just plain lying.*

"Of course you do. Arnie laughed when I called him because he had been afraid that it was a coffin with Will's remains in it. He said you and the sheriff told him that wasn't how the army does it. He wanted to know if I got it all right."

Poppy was trying to figure out whether to make up a story or whether to leave the house and go threaten Arnie for not keeping his mouth shut. He was too slow.

"Here's another of Will's love letters, Poppy." She began to read:

14 June, Portsmouth: Virginia, Peter is dead. A major in the 8th AF confirmed it to me as Peter's next of kin. He crashed somewhere around Carentan. I don't know more than that.

I don't know what will happen to me next but Virginia, I've had to make a decision. Peter is gone and I'm alone. That's the plain truth. I love you with all my heart but I know you don't feel the same about me — you haven't written in months. The only one who told me you were waiting for me was the voice in my head and now the voice finally told me to grow up and quit thinking you were waiting. You never really said you would and seven years is enough. I'm going to stop looking out the bus window to see if you're there. I've got to do something useful with myself. I love you, and that's why I'm not asking you to wait anymore. You're free.

— Will

"Do you understand what I just read? Peter is dead."

"Who's Peter?"

"Will's brother," she screamed at him. "Will's brother."

"And so Will has quit you?"

"His brother is dead. Will sent Peter's things to me in a box that you and the sheriff stole."

"Will can't just quit you, Virginia. This isn't high school. You're pregnant. And you're married."

"Only in your newspaper am I married to Will Hastings, Poppy. Will doesn't know anything about it — the last letter he wrote was July 19, almost a month ago. And he sent it to Virginia Sullivan. Will is the only one who doesn't know that you made that announcement up the minute you found out I was pregnant. And no one believes it. No one."

Poppy glared at her. He wondered why he had ever thought Virginia was anything like her mother; the one thing Emma never did was talk back to him. He had been right all along — Bart was going to turn out just fine but Virginia — she never did what he told her to do and she never would.

"As for Bart, he's just a common thief, weaseling around to pry out every little secret of everyone's lives, then waiting until he can use it. I didn't even get Will's letters, not for as long as you encouraged Bart to try to set up his own little rackets. Or was that you, Poppy, you and Bart sneaking around together with your grand little schemes, printing phony ration cards and helping everyone hide things from the government? You think I can't see with my own eyes, all the extra meat over at Reilly's and the gasoline at Homer's and even the bicycle tires for the kids, just to keep their parents in line? You think I don't know what you're up to? Well, Poppy, if you and Bart had just had the decency to let me have my own letters none of this would have happened."

"Don't you accuse me — you don't know anything about what I do. And you're the one who worked in the ration office. And as for Will's brother, well, too bad. It's war. I didn't see you crying and taking on over Johnny Bradley. You need to learn to take the long view. You're alive. Will is safe. When this is over you two will have your nice little house and you'll have a nice rich husband and all the nice little kids you want."

Poppy knew he was losing control, something he rarely did. But he couldn't stop.

"And me? Who took you to buy all your little booties and bottles and a high chair? And that bed? Huh? Who? What have I got? Nothing. Not a damned thing. Not even my own son. So listen to me Miss High and Mighty, unless and until you tell me where they took my boy, I don't care what happened to your box or Will's brother or anything else. Otherwise, SHUT UP!" he screamed at her.

At that moment, Virginia was ready to tell him the rest. *Fine, Poppy. But don't ask if you don't want to know.* She opened her mouth to begin.

For his part, Poppy was about to slap her. *Just a few times, for her own good.* But, he didn't want to hurt his grandchild, already a week overdue, and with that idiot Pritchard off on a drunk. Besides, he needed to find Hoskins and straighten a few things out. *And Arnie, too. And that god damned Lorena Tarlton.*

However, neither of them got that far. The deafening roar of the B-24 shook the house to its foundations. The laboring high pitch of the propellers, engines at full throttle, beat the air so fiercely that not a sound could be heard anywhere in Tierra or in the fields and pastures that surrounded the town. Whatever Virginia tried to yell at her father was lost in the noise; the turbulence from the airplanes shook her so badly that she began to cramp. Poppy saw her slump to the floor and lowered his fists.

"You're too low," the instructor said into the intercom. "Climb and go around."

As the pilots responded, the bombardier straightened up and looked away from the bomb sight. The engineer closed the bomb bay doors. The plane climbed to two thousand feet above the bleak farm land, turned, and circled back to make a second pass. Two miles west of the town, he spoke again.

"Highest structure, one-hundred-fifty feet above ground. Descend to?"

"Three hundred."

"Right. Direction?"

"Ninety degrees, due east, straight to the water tower."

"Right. Next?"

"Open bomb doors. Turn to one-hundred-seventy, almost due south, to the IP."

As he spoke, the plane roared back over the town, just clearing the water tower, blowing the leaves off the elm trees and kicking dirt up on every street and vacant lot.

"You've got it," the instructor said. He turned to face the student bombardier.

"I've got it," the student replied. He focused into the Norden bombsight and took control of the airplane. In seconds the cemetery came into view, slightly off course to the right. He made a slight adjustment on the bomb-sight and the entire aircraft turned by an increment to line up on the IP, the initial point. He adjusted the view finder for three-hundred-feet above ground level.

"Aiming point!" He shouted into the intercom as the cemetery came into view at the top of the bomb sight. "Pond!" He gripped the bomb release, flipped back the safety, and put his thumb on the firing button.

"Target! Target!"

Click.

"Away! Away! Away!"

The pilots retook control of the airplane. The engines strained as the plane jerked into a steep vertical climb and banked hard to evade anti-aircraft fire from the ball bearing factory. The instructor, the belly gunner, and the aft gunner watched as a dozen sand-filled bomb casings dropped, some brushing trees, two into the quarry, one hitting the earth dam, and four blowing the walls off the shed where Poppy and Hoskins had stored their goods for the last three years.

Not everyone in Tierra heard the dummies hit the target area, but from the platform on top of the windmill Sandy and Sluggo did. "I heard the army pays three dollars to finders." They jumped on their bicycles and rode as hard as they could to the cemetery, then began to run across the fields in search of bomb casings.

They were too late. By the time they got to the bluff they could see that the roof had collapsed diagonally, pulling down the walls nearest the quarry pond and knocking the doors off the hinges. The far walls leaned at a wild angle, tilting precariously away from the wreckage like a homemade raft launched over a waterfall. Boxes, bales, pallets, and tarpaulins were scattered all over the earth floor, cluttered on top of each other, torn, broken, and smashed beyond use. And there, in the wreckage of cigarettes, tires, and the rest, stood Sheriff Hoskins, kicking at the shattered remains of his and Poppy's contraband. The only thing that appeared to have been left intact was the motor. Sandy knew what the motor was.

"It's the Bessemer combustion engine. See the flywheels? And the lead pipes?" he whispered to Sluggo, pointing through the trees.

"How do you know that?" Sluggo whispered back.

"Because my dad was in charge of it. At the cotton gin, before it burned down. I used to see it all the time."

Neither of them questioned how the engine had escaped the fire; such things happened in an adult world. In a child's world, however, Sandy couldn't wait to get home to tell his mother, and he already knew exactly what he would say:

"Mom! The cotton gin engine — it's okay! Dad'll be coming home soon."

"Good morning, Lorena."

"Why goodness Mr. Bradley, you startled me." She had been kneeling on the floor of the post office, her key inserted into the oversized mail box. Bradley had walked in so quietly that she hadn't heard him. "I was going to send Sandy over with your mail in just a few minutes."

"Oh, Sandy won't be along this morning. In fact, I just talked to him. About that plane that came over so low yesterday. So I thought I'd get my mail myself. For a change."

"Oh, no need to do that. Just run on back to the barber shop; I'll have it over in five minutes."

"No, like I said. I'll get it myself."

She moved sideways on her knees to block the box. He squatted down on the floor beside her.

"Why, I must be losing my mind, Mr. Bradley. I don't think I remembered to bring the key. Let me just run home and get it. I'll send Sandy over with your mail in just a few minutes."

"No need for that, Lorena. Let's just have the postmaster get it."

He was not surprised by the look of panic on her face, nor did it stop him. He stood up, walked around the corner to the window, and called for the postmaster.

"Hello. Good morning. I'm John Bradley. Mrs. Tarlton usually gets my mail but she seems to have forgotten the key this morning. May I have everything in my box, please?"

"Number?"

"Box 12. Right around there on the bottom."

"Sure. Big one. Be right back."

"Here you are," he said, handing Mr. Bradley the bills for barber supplies and advertisements. "And these. You know, these have been in that box ever since I've been here. Wondered if you were ever going pick them up."

He handed Bradley two large envelopes, thick, wrapped in plain brown paper, the size of books.

"Thank you, Sir. Thank you kindly."

Bradley turned to leave and noticed that Lorena Tarlton had already fled. There was no doubt in his mind that Sandy had been right, that the Bessemer engine in the shed had been taken out of the cotton gin. He also figured that someone had done it before the fire.

He went directly to the barber shop, unlocked the door, entered, and locked it again behind him. He left the 'Closed' sign in the window and did not turn on the lights. Instead, he went into the back room, the broom closet and pinup gallery, pulled on the chain to illuminate the bare bulb above the doorway, and began to unwrap the first of the two envelopes.

He looked at the cotton certificates, noticed the dates, the farmers' names.

Well, it's already eight-fifteen in the morning; maybe she's found the sonofabitch already, maybe not.

He put the envelopes high up on the shelf, behind the towels and the bottles of Barbasol and dry soap, then covered them. He stepped out, locked the closet, then went out the front door and locked it. It was no more than a half block around the corner to the telephone exchange.

"Good morning, Miss Somerville. Need you to place a call for me."

"What number?" She sat at a cramped desk, the switchboard visible behind her, rows of plugs and wires on jacks at the ready. She took up a pencil and paper and paused, waiting for the number Mr. Bradley would have her dial.

"Don't rightly know, Ma'am. But it's a government office. In Lubbock."

"I can look it up. What office?"

"I suppose it's the FBI."

"Well, that's exciting. Go over to number one." She pointed to three telephones mounted on the wall, each numbered. "When it rings, pick up the telephone."

He waited and, when number one rang, he looked at her. She nodded. Bradley picked up the telephone and began to talk.

CHAPTER TWELVE

Labor Day

Virginia awoke in the middle of the night and knew instinctively that something was wrong. She could sense that the house was empty but went from room to room to check. Poppy's door was open, the bed not been slept in. Poppy had taken to sitting in Bart's room, on the bed, waiting, as if Bart would come through the door any minute and brag about another escapade of girls in Clovis or of fruit jars of brandy sold to some high school kids. She opened Bart's door; his room too was vacant. She moved on to the front door and opened it wide enough to look through the screen. The Ford was not outside.

She called the telephone exchange at six in the morning and asked for the sheriff's office. A sleepy jailer told her that he didn't know anything about Poppy, but not to worry. *Him and the Sheriff's always goin' off. He'll turn up.* No one had told the jailer anything and there was nothing among the scraps of paper on the desk that looked like the sheriff had been called out on an accident or anything like that.

She was cramping again. After a week she feared that it was no longer just the result of having been shaken by loud airplanes. She called Miss Somerville again and asked if she would wake Doc Pritchard. He didn't answer the telephone.

As soon as it was light, she dressed and walked to the center of town.

The lights were out at the *Tierra Times*. Poppy's car was not there. She tried to peer through the windows but the Venetian blinds had been turned so that she could not make anything out past the front counter.

From the *Times* she walked to the post office. The front door was unlocked, as usual, but there was no one inside and the lights in the back were still off. She turned to leave but, more by reflex than thought process, she looked in the Sullivan mail box. Through the glass window in the box door she could make out the shape of an envelope, so she dialed the combination.

There was a letter from Will. Her first instinct was to wait until later. Something was wrong; Poppy and Doc both were missing and the people who should know about them were no help. Her second instinct was to pause and read the letter. She opened it.

20 July — Still in Ste. Marie and have to hurry. The unit left an hour ago but I stayed behind to check on a boy who Collins had taken care of, a GSW in the leg. He was sent back to the evac. hospital five days ago but when I got back here some of the men told me that they wanted me to check on a soldier in the barn that someone at Isigny had returned to duty and sure enough it was the same boy, named Newton. He was dead. The gunshot wound looked like someone had injected the muscle full of pain killer and he probably didn't feel it when it got infected until it was too late. I think this is the boy Antsley had tried to put back on sick call and someone at Division Medical Office overruled us. If I had seen him yesterday I could have gotten him back to the evacuation hospital and also told them that some administrative officer somewhere F/W medical treatment. Instead, I'm being sent away to look at a site for a new hospital. SSDD. I'm sending this to you just in case. — Will

She read it a second time, quickly. *My God they're in the middle of a war where doctors are killing people and here I am four thousand miles away, about to have a baby in a cotton town where the only doctor is a drunk, and he's disappeared.*

Virginia knew this time that she really was alone, and she was scared.

Virginia went back home. She tried to make a pot of coffee, something to help her settle down while she decided what she could do. She looked around at the new rocking chair, the baby bed, all the little socks and bibs. *It's Poppy,* she thought. *He always told me where to sit, what to do, how to dress. He made a mess of my life and now I look up and he isn't here and I don't know what to do.*

At eight she called the exchange again and asked for Nona's Café out on the highway. No, no one had seen Poppy, or Doc either for that matter. They hadn't been by last night or this morning, but Nona would call if she heard anything. She got the same answer at the cotton co-op, at Franklin's Hardware store, at the depot. She decided against calling Mrs. Tarlton. *The old bitch was probably listening on the party line anyway.*

At nine she went into Poppy's bedroom and rummaged around in his dresser until she found his key ring. At nine-fifteen she walked back to the *Times* and tried the keys, one after the other. At nine-twenty she found the right key and opened the door.

"Exchange. This is Virginia again. No, I haven't. I'm over at the newspaper now. Listen, this is urgent. Let me talk to the sheriff." She waited a minute before a voice came on. "Hello. This is Virginia Sullivan. Hastings. Virginia. I'm over at the newspaper. Poppy's still missing and it looks like somebody broke in here. I think they robbed him. Hurry. Can you come over?"

The jailer was the only one on duty. He locked up the outer steel door and told both of the drunks that they would have to wait for breakfast. He passed the judge out in the hallway.

"Morning, Your Honor. I'm locking up the sheriff's office; something wrong over at the paper."

When he got there Virginia was sitting on the only chair. Around her, on the floor, there were the large trays of lead type, dumped and scattered. Rolls of paper had been ripped from the press and lay scrolled across the room. Poppy's desk had been emptied; not a single sheet of paper or note was to be found.

"Well, girl. This don't look good. Where's your dad?"

She reminded him that she had called him three hours earlier and asked him the same question. He scratched his head.

"So, when did you find this?"

She told him that she had found the spare key and opened the door just after nine o'clock, then called him.

They checked the back door as well; it was locked from the inside and did not appear to have been opened. Even Virginia could tell that whomever had wrecked the *Tierra Times* had come in through the front door, with a key, and locked up when they left.

"What was there?" He pointed to an empty table. Dust and ink marks outlined a square on the table top, the outline of a machine that had been on there a long time.

"I don't remember," she fibbed. Someone had taken the small color ink composer. Poppy had bought it three years before to set up and print small runs of color advertisements. The only thing remaining was a mocked up Sunday ad for Reilly's Grocery, the red lettering the same color as meat ration stamps, the blue exactly the same as sugar rations. The jailer paid no attention to it.

"I say we gotta lock this place back up and wait until Sheriff Hoskins comes in. He's going to have to investigate this, Girl. This is way more than I can do."

That was when they both realized that Sheriff Hoskins hadn't been seen since the night before, either. They picked up the telephone and called the exchange. After ten rings it was clear that Hoskins was not going to answer his home telephone.

The jailer had decided to drive over to the Sheriff's house when a noise startled them. From the back of the office a machine began to clatter, then type. The wire service was sending in the day's first news report.

As she had done in the post office, Virginia went back to check on it, more from habit than choice. The wire clattered noisily for a few minutes. Clipped stories of baseball scores, meat shortages, and war bond drives pecked their way across the scrolling pages. The General Motors factory had delivered more airplanes to the military in the month of June than in all of 1943. Marines were locked in battle on Guam. Rommel was dead. Hitler was conducting mock trials of the men he thought had tried to assassinate him.

Then came the casualty lists:

· ·

/// OWI/// 15 Aug 44////

The Secretary has released the following names to the Associated Press. Local news organizations should confirm with families before publication.

Texas:.....

Hamm, Rocky, Amarillo, KIA

Haney, Luther, San Antonio, missing,

Hancock, Roland, Dallas, missing,

Hanson, John, Laredo, KIA
Hastings, Will, Tierra, WIA

The jailer heard her fall but was too late to catch her. She hit her head on the chair and landed on the trays of newspaper type and scattered lead. He gaped at her pregnant belly rolled to one side, her legs splayed underneath her and jammed against the trays on the floor.

"'Ginia? 'Ginia? You okay?" He pinched her cheeks and patted her hands, then found the telephone.

"Exchange, you gotta call Doc Pritchard." Pause. "Yeah, he's got to get over here to the paper! Now! Yes! Poppy's girl! She's knocked out on the floor here!" Pause. "I don't know. Looks bad to me. Hurry!"

Shirley Fleming was uncomfortable. She sat in the wooden chair, squirmed, moving her bottom as discretely as she could to find a better fit, then adjusted her skirt to cover her legs. Once settled, she discovered that the wooden back jammed rudely into her shoulder blade. She shifted again and both the seat and the back pushed against uncomfortable parts. She looked to either side; there were only more wooden chairs. It occurred to her that the sofa was more likely to be comfortable but she could not imagine a circumstance in which she could be induced to move over and sit on it.

"You'd think in a place like this there would be more consideration for the public."

Hoyt glanced at Shirley, politely, uncertain whether she expected him to do something for her consideration as a member of the public. He found it odd that someone could complain about sitting in a chair. He understood, just from watching, that she had picked the chair to avoid him.

He didn't answer.

She sat on the chair to make it harder for him to stare at her without making a fool of himself. The chair was on the same side of the waiting room as he was, not opposite, but with a divan in between. If she had sat opposite he could have stared at her all evening, which would have been even more annoying. She was prepared to show Hoyt Carter just how annoyed she could be. Her rudeness to him was like riding a bicycle, something she had perfected in high school when Hoyt used to peek at her from over his book and gaze at her in the cafeteria. Back then, when the six of them went to Nona's or the picture show together, Hoyt used to try to make it like he and Shirley were on dates. They had never been on a date, not as far as she was concerned.

Now, by rapidly peeking from the side of her eyes, she saw that he rarely glanced at her. He sat quietly, erect, and waited. She sneaked another look — he was as stoic as a chieftan. That annoyed her as much as if he had stared at her the way he used to do, years before, when they were just kids. After a half hour of silence, she gave up.

"So, Hoyt, guess you found everything changed, huh?"

"Ah, naw, not really," he answered. "Well, yes, I guess you're right. My little brother — when I saw him last, he was just this big." Hoyt held his hand about shoulder high to show how big. "Now, Jim Ned's almost as tall as I am, and Nell — you should just see her. They changed all right. But the farm, to tell you the truth, it looked exactly like I remembered it."

What had changed had been in town. It seemed to Hoyt that not many people were left in Tierra. He was used to there being a lot of people, even in the jungle. Now, after years of absence, Tierra seemed very small and very dry, remote, almost uninhabited.

"I'm just glad to be home. Well, not for long. I have to go back in a couple of days."

"So, you must have thought a lot about it while you were over there, huh?"

"About what?"

"How you would get home and find that everything's changed."

He hadn't.

"Oh, mostly I just thought about getting home. I never thought anything would change. Home isn't supposed to change; it's supposed to be the way it was when you left it."

"Well, have you looked around town?" Shirley thought everything had changed. "There's nobody left. The boys all get drafted soon as they're old enough. A lot of the men go over to Seminole, even down as far as Odessa, to work in the oil fields. And the stores! They're all empty. No new clothes, sugar, not even any shoes. It's hard to buy anything. It's the war."

Hoyt hadn't been in a store in three years. For two of those three years he had hidden in trees and caves. It had not occurred to him to look for new clothes or sugar.

"I guess you're right," he answered. "I didn't think about that much, I suppose."

"What did you think about?" She expected him to say "you," but he didn't. Instead, he waited so long before he answered that she started to ask again.

"Mostly I thought about Mr. Bradley." He let out a breath of air, not a sigh, more like he had been holding his breath for a long time. "I knew before I talked to him that it was going to hurt him a lot. I told him that I wished it had been me, but that didn't make it any better. And I knew that it wouldn't."

She didn't know what to say about that, and said nothing.

They had not said much in the pickup. It had taken almost an hour to drive from Tierra to Clovis and she and Hoyt had both been afraid that something would happen that they wouldn't know how to handle. Virginia had sat between them, doubled over in the seat, then arching backward, then letting out such painful sounds that Shirley cringed. Hoyt had driven as fast as he could and with the mistaken belief that Shirley was trying to help her best friend.

She should have told him, when Sandy had come to the front door and told her that Hoyt was outside asking for her, to go away. When Hoyt himself called at her to come out and get in the pickup she hadn't realized that it was because he didn't know what to do with Virginia in labor. For the entire time it took to drive to Clovis, Shirley had wanted to tell him to stop the truck and let her out, but she didn't have the courage. She decided that when they got to the hospital she would tell the attendants that she was not supposed to be there. *Now, if you don't mind, I'll just sit in the lobby and wait until Hoyt leaves her with the nurses, and we'll be on our way. That's what I'm going to tell them.*

Hoyt would have been surprised to know what she was thinking. When he had found the small adobe Clovis Hospital and Clinic he skidded the pickup to a halt, jumped out, and ran up the steps to the hospital. Within moments he came back with two nurses who told Shirley to get out of the way. She had stepped to the side, ignored, while the nurses helped Virginia get out of the pickup. She stood on the sidewalk while someone brought a wheelchair, then waited alone while Virginia and Hoyt and the nurses disappeared back into the hospital. No one had asked Shirley what she was doing there.

After a few minutes she had walked into the clinic, found the lobby, and perched on a chair. *I'll tell them I need to use the telephone,* she told herself. *The first person to come out here, I'll tell them. I'll call Mother.*

The first person to come into the lobby had been Hoyt and he didn't appear until late in the evening. There was no one in the office. Hoyt told her with evident relief that "they" had Virginia.

"The nurses said there's nothing to do but wait. We'll just wait here, Shirley. I'm used to waiting. We'll just wait right here." That had been an hour ago.

"Like I said, I guess you noticed that it's pretty dead," she continued. "The town."

"Mostly I've just stayed out at the farm. Well, we came in to church once. That was Sunday. That was a change, you know. I haven't really been to church…" He trailed off.

Shirley disapproved of this.

"Well I don't see why. The war doesn't stop us from going to church and there's no reason why it should stop the men in uniform. In fact, the men in uniform should be the ones who go to church most."

She told him that and, as soon as she did, she saw a look on his face. He didn't look hurt or reprimanded the way she used to make him look years before. This look was something else, something she couldn't put her finger on.

He didn't answer her. He nodded, instead, and maintained his polite smile while seemingly looking at nothing more than the pale green hospital wall.

"I'm sorry, Hoyt. I shouldn't have said that."

"No, it's fine. It's just, well, you know, there aren't any churches there. I guess I didn't think about it much, not until I got home and then Ma brought us in to church. I was just saying that I haven't seen much of the town yet, just the church. And Mr. Bradley. Then today I came in to town and went over to the Sullivans to ask about Will.

That caused her to listen more carefully to Hoyt.

"Did Virginia have any news? Of Will, I mean?"

"Well, I don't know. She wasn't home so I went looking and I saw this boy who said he thought she was at the paper. So when I got there she was on the floor and looking pretty bad. So before we even got to talk about Will or anything I said 'Are you okay?' and she didn't answer me and I said 'Do you want me to take you to Doc Pritchard?' and she started kind of crying like, and she said he wasn't there any more."

Shirley started to tell Hoyt the gossip, then remembered that her father had told her and her mother and Butch to not discuss it. At dinner, twenty-four hours after the bomber had successfully demolished the shed at the quarry, Butch Fleming told his parents everything he and Sandy and Tommy and Sluggo had seen inside the shed. To Shirley's surprise her father had said, with a degree of earnestness, "There are rumors going around about the Sheriff and Mr. Sullivan." He had paused, taken a sip of his iced tea, then continued, "And I think it's best if we just don't talk about it at all. To anyone."

Butch, however, was not accustomed to paying much attention to his father. He continued to talk about seeing tires, shoes, cigarettes, and "A Bessemer Type IV engine. Sandy Clayton says it's the one from the gin."

It was the first time in her life that Shirley had seen her father lose his temper. "Stop right now. Not another word! I order you! And you and you!" he had said to each of them, "to never say one word of that business of the shed to anyone. Not one word!"

For the first time in family memory, the Flemings did as Mr. Fleming had told them. Butch's observations did not leave the family table.

"I didn't know what to do, Shirley, her being in bad shape and all. I've seen some things but I don't know that I could deliver a baby. There was a deputy there and he said could I bring her to the hospital and then Virginia sort of came to and said for me to come get you. That's why I came to your house." He paused and, for the first time, looked directly at Shirley. "I am sorry you got dragged off over here."

Ever since she heard that Hoyt Carter had somehow made it home from the war, Shirley had manufactured the belief that he had willed himself to escape those horrid Japanese solely to come back to Tierra and beg her to give him a chance. She sat at her bureau and read film magazines and disagreed with her mother about what to take from the garden for dinner, all the while quietly planning how she would refuse to "see" Hoyt. It had not been in her plans that three weeks would go by before he came to beg and by this morning she had become impatient. Then, there he was.

Now, sitting in the hospital's hard wooden chair, cloaked by a pile of old magazines and the smell of disinfectant, she admitted to herself that she had opened the door two hours ago only because it had been part of an elaborate plan. *If he thinks Will Hastings rejected me, I'll set him straight. And if he thinks I have to settle for him, I'll set him even straighter.* Butch had told her that Hoyt's leave was up and he would be going back to the Army. She could send him away again, ever the unattainable prize. She had planned and memorized the words she would use to tell him that he still was not good enough for her. She would agree to let him sit in the living room and talk, if her mother was home, but only about army life and life here on the home front, victory gardens and war bonds. Then, when he asked her to walk to the drug store or up to Nona's for a Coke or a cup of coffee, she would say *Oh, Hoyt, you're sweet but no, thanks. This isn't like we're going to the movies with Johnny and Molly and Will. I don't want to lead you on.* She would have carefully excluded any reference to Virginia in the memories she would permit Hoyt to have of their days in high school. *Let's just be friends. I don't want to go out with you.* Then she would walk him to the front door and watch his hurt look as he went away, just as he had done the last time she had been too good for him and he had run off to join the army. It had never occurred to Shirley that the only reason Hoyt came to her house was because Virginia had asked him to get Shirley to help. *That was not very thoughtful of Virginia.*

"I thought you were just coming by to see me," she answered.

"Well, that's real nice Shirley. For you to think I was coming by."

It also hadn't occurred to her, and was only now beginning to occur to her, that Hoyt wasn't Hoyt. The soldier who been outside in the Carter's farm truck was not chubby. He was washed, very clean shaved, and his hair trimmed. The creases of his uniform were straight and crisp. And he had been very clear and plainspoken: "Shirley, come with me. Hurry." His voice had been so commanding that she hadn't hesitated to get in the truck and she had forgotten all about her planned speeches. Hoyt had changed.

Hoyt Carter had been home twice since they had graduated from high school. His first leave lasted long enough for him to help get the cotton in, work the litters of pigs, and go to church once. After church, Shirley had sent him away. Six months later he had come home for a week before he and Johnny shipped out to Hawaii. Mrs. Fleming informed Hoyt that Shirley was at Texas Tech. He had sent her a post card once, a Kodak Color Card, of palm trees arching over the beach, the blue ocean lapping the sand. Hula girls swayed in the breeze. Bronzed men glided on tall surf boards. The word 'paradise' was printed on the sky in yellow. "Johnny and me are here in Paradise. Wish you could see it." He had written his Army service number and unit address on the card. She never wrote back.

Hoyt had asked about her a few times in his letters home. Then he and Johnny were sent to the Philippines. A week after Hoyt watched the Japanese shoot Johnny Bradley in the back of the head he strangled a guard and slipped into the jungle. He found the Filippino Scouts and they found him. They taught him to walk without leaving a trail, to sleep in the crooks of mahogany trees and to eat snakes. He had learned to eat rice and drink boiled tea. The risk of noise from a gun shot was so great that firing a rifle was reserved for shooting Japanese soldiers from great distances and from the concealment of hidden trees and stream beds. The only women Hoyt had seen for three years had been on the verge of starvation.

Sometime, he had no idea when, maybe in 1940 or maybe in 1941, or after Pearl Harbor, after Wake Island, after Corregidor or Bataan, he forgot her. Now, when he saw Shirley Fleming for the first time in years, he thought she was unusually large and curiously impolite. Even back in Hawaii, in the paradise of hula girls and army nurses, the women had been very small. Shirley was not fat, or stocky, or even large, but neither had she suffered much from rationing on the home front.

"You were coming to see me, weren't you?"

"Sure I was, Shirley," he lied.

She pouted briefly.

"Why did you go see Virginia first?"

"Will."

"Will's off in France. But I'm here."

What would have irritated most men did not irritate Hoyt. He knew exactly what had happened to Johnny but he didn't know what had happened to Will. Virginia would know. It was no more complicated than that.

"I was hoping she could tell me what kind of outfit he was in, or where he was. It makes a big difference. And I wondered if she could tell me about Molly. I don't know where to find her. I don't suppose you could tell me, could you?"

Shirley still wanted her father to come get her but not a single nurse or anyone else had come to the frosted glass office window. Shirley got up and walked to it, then slid open the glass open.

"Hello? Is anybody there?"

No one answered from the darkened desk area. The door behind the desk was closed.

"Hoyt, what are they doing back there?"

Of Virginia they heard nothing.

He misunderstood her anxiety.

"She'll be fine, Shirley. The nurses were real nice and everybody seemed to know what they were doing."

"What takes them so long? You were back there an hour, and we've been here all day."

"It's funny. They thought I was her husband. Virginia wasn't making much sense of it. She looked pretty bad and they put her up on a little table and rolled her through some doors. Most of the time I was just waiting back there until one of the nurses told me the husbands waited out here. I had to tell her I wasn't her husband, and she said she wondered why I brought her here instead of out to the base hospital. She told me just to wait here and they would come out to tell me any news."

The day became evening. To her question of why Hoyt had been singled out to drive Virginia to the hospital, and not Poppy, he told her that it looked like the newspaper office had been robbed, that the only ones there were Virginia and a deputy. They talked about Bart's disappearance but neither seemed surprised that Doc had gone missing.

At seven in the evening they heard her.

Virginia's first scream was electrifying. Shirley had general ideas about the pains of childbirth but no first-hand experience. The sound that punched into the room, under the door, through the frosted glass window, and seemingly through the solid walls themselves had begun at Virginia's ripped and dilated nether parts and traveled up her spinal canal, gathering strength as it emerged into her sinuses and teeth and the backs of her lips where it burst out in a shriek that only mothers and nurses could tolerate, a pain so fierce that Shirley envisioned broken glass and alcohol and the teeth of rats and sharp spikes ripping flesh away from well-connected bones and tissues. The scream held, then descended to a yell, and then to a moan before it disappeared, leaving only shock.

"Hoyt, …"

"That was Virginia, I'm pretty sure," he answered.

"Is she…" Shirley trailed off, aware that no one was going to come out to the waiting room to see if she needed anything.

"Hoyt, I don't think anyone knows where I am. Would you drive me back to Tierra? Please?"

"And leave Virginia? You don't want to wait with her….?"

Somehow, Shirley didn't know how, his questions made her feel accused, and she felt guilty. *Of course I want to leave her here. No, I don't want to wait. I certainly do want to go home and leave that harlot to sleep in the bed she made for herself; it isn't my affair.* But the note of surprise in his voice had the same mixture of disbelief and abandonment that she knew herself, from standing at the steps of Will's bus and watching him disappear.

"She'll be all right — this is a hospital."

Hoyt didn't answer her, not out loud. Instead she saw his mouth form a wry smile, cheeks flattened and eyes perceptibly wider, and she understood that Hoyt Carter had concluded that she was not a good person. Her instinct was to blame him — he didn't know what she had put up with. It was the old Hoyt again, who didn't understand what it was like to be robbed of someone you cared about by someone you hated. Then it hit her.

Hoyt's here; Johnny isn't. Hoyt knows more about losing someone than I ever will. And for the first time in her life, Shirley wondered if maybe somewhere in her life she had gotten off the track and was waking up to find that she was on the wrong train. She had no idea where Molly was, had never asked about Johnny, and was trying to punish Hoyt for the simple act of being Will's friend. She sat on her hands, concentrated, and gathered her courage, then asked.

"Hoyt, would you like to tell me about Johnny?"

He was shaking his head when Virginia screamed again, sharper, but with less of the note of betrayal and surprise that her first deep labor pain had brought out.

"That was about six or eight minutes," Hoyt said. "It'll take a while, I'm afraid."

She knew that she would not ask Hoyt to drive her home.

From the corner of her eye she studied him. Hoyt was taller than she remembered, and thinner. He sat quietly, his posture erect. His hair was neatly combed, his army boots well-polished. The chevrons on his sleeves set off the developed muscles of his arms. His uniform was not tight nor did his stomach sag or stick out. He had folded his Army cap and buttoned it under the shoulder epaulets of his uniform. If she had not known Hoyt Carter from twelve grades of school, she would have thought he was a nice man. She lowered the magazine.

"What do those mean? Those ribbons?" She pointed at the row on his shirt pocket. "I know they're awards or something. But what do they mean?"

"Aw, I don't know. Everybody has them. You wake up one day and someone gives them to you. Then you have to get them sewed onto your uniform."

"I don't believe you. You're being modest. Tell me"

"They aren't anything. Really. Like this one — I was in the hospital, that's all." He pointed to a purple ribbon. "And it was them, not me. They made me stay in there for a long time. There wasn't anything wrong with me, just lost a little weight. Anyway, when they said I could go, they issued me some new uniforms. There wasn't anything left of the old ones anymore. Well, when I put my new shirt on they had already sewed these stripes on the sleeves. They never said anything to me about it. But sure enough, when my orders come through to come home, they said I was a sergeant."

"And those? What are they? She pointed to three decorations on his chest.

"Ah, just ribbons. One says I was in the Philippines. This one says I was in combat or something. This other one I think they give to everybody." The other one was an orange ribbon with vertical colored stripes and a bronze star pendant below, a decoration for combat with uncommon valor. "The Army just likes ribbons, I think. They don't mean much."

"What was it like, there in the Philippines? Did you see Canaan?"

"Canaan?"

"Yes, or Gaza?"

"I guess not. I don't remember hearing about any places like that."

"Oh, Hoyt, that's a shame. That's where Samson was. Samson and Delilah. It would have been real nice to see where he met Delilah, and where she cut his hair. And the temple where he pulled the pillars down because they put out his eyes."

"Who?"

"The Philistines. They put Samson's eyes out when Delilah cut his hair, and then God gave him one wish and he wished for strength to get revenge for being blinded and he pulled the pillars of the temple down on the Philistines. You were there for all that time and didn't get to see it. That would have been something."

Hoyt realized, not for the last time, that Shirley had memorized too many Bible verses without learning the lesson.

"I didn't see any Philistines."

"They must have all been gone. That's because of Samson. I wish you could have seen it; I would have liked you to tell me about it."

He smiled politely, then resumed gazing at the soothing green walls of the lobby. The fluorescent lights gave off a low grade hum which sounded like the mosquitos on the grass flats of the Pulangi. He wondered what

Shirley would think about eating bony fish from a stick or running barefoot through the tall grass to escape a crocodile only to see a Japanese foot patrol a hundred yards upriver. He had told her that there wasn't anything wrong with him in the hospital because she would probably tell all the ladies in town, and sooner or later his mother would hear he had malaria. Everyone had malaria; no one here needed to know about that, or the dynamite either. Or the submarine. He would never tell Shirley about them, that's for sure, no more than he would tell Mr. Bradley about watching them murder Johnny in a ditch by a dirt track in the jungle on the first day after the surrender. He smiled politely and listened to the hum of the lights. His mother didn't need any more scares. A nurse came in.

"Sergeant Sullivan?" She walked over to Hoyt, who stood up.

"No, Ma'am. I'm Sergeant Carter."

"Are you the soldier who brought in Mrs. Sullivan?"

"Yes, Ma'am. Her friend here and I brought her in. Is she okay? I mean, with, you know?" Hoyt did not know precisely what he was asking. That he had seen many things on the Carter farm and other things on Mindinao did not mean he had seen a woman in the final stages of giving birth.

"She's fine. She'll be with us a while. Can you tell us some things for the chart? The office will fix it up when they come in the morning, but we've got to start a chart for her."

"I'll do what I can. Sure."

"Her name is Virginia Sullivan?"

"Yes. No. It was, but it's Hastings now. She married my friend, Will Hastings."

Shirley sat upright in the wooden chair and listened. *Oh no,* she thought. *I have to say something.* Hoyt did not notice.

"Where's he?"

"Somewhere in France. He's in the army. He's a doctor, too. An Army doctor. Real nice fellow."

"So this is an army baby. We don't get many of those. Most of them go over to the army air base west of town. They've got their own infirmary over there. Why didn't she go there?"

"I don't know, Ma'am. I went to their newspaper office and there was a deputy who said to bring her to the hospital here. Her people have all disappeared. Even her doctor disappeared."

The nurse tried to keep up with Hoyt's rambling stories. She listened while he explained that Virginia was a real nice girl. "I've been knowing her since she was in first grade. And Will, too. That's Captain Hastings. Did you know he made captain, Shirley? And Will too, since high school."

"He was in ninth grade when he came here, Hoyt."

"Yes, Ma'am. Ninth grade. And they were always good friends and you know, then I went off and joined the army and I was away when he was in school. He went to the army, too, and so I really didn't get to talk to either one of them until today. But my parents told me they eloped after Thanksgiving because he was home on leave and just about to get shipped out. Then, when I got over to the newspaper — her dad owns the paper there — and when I got over there she had fallen down and it looked like she started, I guess, you know. And now Will's in France and she's, well, she's right here."

"Birthday?"

"Her birthday? I don't rightly know. Shirley, do you know her birthday? You girls were always having parties like that. We didn't have parties like that but you girls did. What's Virginia's birthday, Shirley?"

Shirley didn't know. The nurse wrote 1920. Hoyt was born in 1920. Shirley too was born in 1920. 1920 sounded about right.

"And the father?"

"Will? That's Captain Hastings, he's the father, like I said. Is that what you mean?"

She hadn't meant that. She had meant to find out his birthday as well. It was the next item on the form she was filling out. She wrote "Captain Hastings" by the father's name and made a note to ask Miss Sullivan or Mrs. Sullivan or Mrs. Hastings or whatever her name was to tell them the father's birth date and to straighten her own name out. *A lot of these girls with their first babies say all sorts of things.*

Shirley realized that it was then or never to say what she knew about Virginia's marriage to Will Hastings. She formed the words. *They aren't married. Her father ran the paper and when she turned up pregnant he put an announcement in the paper that said they eloped, but he was already off at the war by then. They never eloped.* She faced the clerk, screwed up her courage, and failed.

"Well, he was — is — my best friend, him and Johnny Bradley," Hoyt continued. We were like twins, the three of us."

"Triplets. If there were three of you."

Shirley's mind continued to spin. *I was there. They did not elope, because I was there. When he left he said, "Virginia will you wait for me?" and she never answered him. And then after he left, she...*

"That's right," Hoyt continued. "We were the Three Musketeers, everybody said. Until we all joined the army and now we're not, well, not the Three Musketeer triplets any more."

"I just meant to ask his birth date. Do you know his?"

"No, I sure don't. Shirley?" He startled her. "Shirley, you don't know Will's birthday do you?"

November 27, 1919. She panicked.

"No Ma'am. I'm sorry," Hoyt rambled on. "We don't. I guess you could just put down 1920. Like on Virginia."

The moment passed. Shirley said nothing. *Why,* she asked herself, *why couldn't I tell them? Why did that — that tramp — tell Hoyt to come get me? It's coming out all wrong.*

"I don't suppose you know anything about her blood type?"

"Nope."

"Number of weeks?"

"Not hardly, no Ma'am. We don't know any of that. I'm sorry. Is the baby here?"

"Oh, goodness no."

"When is the baby going to be here? We'll wait."

"Whenever it's ready. Could be now, could be tomorrow, she might go back home. Never know with these new mommas." *In fact,* she thought, *this is going to be a long one.* Virginia was having a tough time and, from the looks of her, the nurses thought she was anemic. A lot of girls had trouble eating what they should, the nurses thought. It was the war.

"Is she — bad? Hurting?" Shirley asked the one question that had been on her mind from the time she realized Virginia was pregnant — how much did it hurt?

"Not bad. It's normal. Everything's normal." *Nothing* you *have to be worried about,* the nurse thought. Shirley wasn't the first spinster to be afraid of that kind of pain. "I'm going back in, now. Nice to meet you. Thanks for the help. I'll let you know." She patted the chart she had been writing on, put on a dutiful smile for the two of them, then turned and walked back into the recesses of the hospital.

Shirley's chance had come and it had passed. The nurse had broken the moment. Shirley knew that she had made a mess about the Philistines. Hoyt knew he couldn't tell her about hiding in the daytime, slipping through the tall grasses of the Cotabato to kill Japanese soldiers on patrol and throwing their bodies to crocodiles. But both of them were aware that for the first time in their lives, Shirley Fleming and Hoyt Carter had spoken with each other, privately, about things that mattered to them. She took a deep breath, and began.

"I really didn't expect to hear from Will, Hoyt. But I thought you might write to me." She was lying, of course, and they both knew it. But it wasn't her lie that mattered, it was her invitation. It surprised her as much as him.

Hoyt was unsure whether to accept or decline. He had been with a few girls here and there, danced in the post exchange club and gone swimming with Hawaiian girls who were so tiny and whose faces were so round and innocent that they looked more like they were twelve than twenty. It was after his escape, in the years on the ground moving and hiding with bands of guerillas in the redoubts of Mindinao, that he had learned to sleep with them. He had coupled for acceptance, affection, and because he could, but Hoyt had never pursued a girl, not in Honolulu, nor in the Philippines, nor afterward when they kept him in Australia. From the moment Johnny died Hoyt wanted to come home, after the war, and never see another tree or mountain or Asian as long as he lived, and there would be no entanglement to stop him. *I guess I've changed a lot*, he thought. *Shirley probably did too.*

"What was it you wanted me to write you?" he answered. He would be patient. He had learned that. "I can tell you now."

The nurses awakened Hoyt and Shirley, asleep in the lobby, to announce that Virginia had given birth to a little boy.

"He's pretty small. And she'll be confined for some time."

At a few minutes past seven Hoyt and Shirley stood before the glass window of the only operating room in the hospital. A nurse drew back the curtains, then held up for them to see Virginia's squalling, angry, and very red-faced infant. Hoyt gazed at the child, studying his every move, his tiny fingers and toes, all thrashing arms and legs and his head wobbling around on the tiny neck. They each declared that it was a good thing the child didn't take on after Poppy; each thought privately that the little stinker was more like Bart.

Shirley gazed at Hoyt, the last person she would have thought would be interested in a baby. Neither of them had ever seen anything quite like it before.

Nona's Café was not more than fifty feet from the Clovis highway, separated from the pavement by a dusty parking lot. It marked the middle of town, the place where cars would turn off the highway to go to the square a few blocks in, or where drivers leaving Tierra would go up the road to get on the highway. By nine o'clock Mrs. Tarlton had taken up her place at the window. She sipped her coffee and thought about the demise of her silent partnership with Poppy Sullivan, now ended. Arnie was there for coffee, chatting with the men who worked in the office of the cotton co-op. Some of the farmers who came into town to pick up supplies huddled on the counter stools, arguing whether the town would be better off with Hoskins in jail over in Lubbock or if he was just the first egg who was going to get broken. All of them knew that there was more cotton in the fields than anyone had ever seen and, if they were going to get it picked, someone needed to start rebuilding the gin. Mr. Fleming had just left for the bank after cautioning them that loose lips could still sink some ships. Some mentioned that it was a good riddance to Doc Pritchard but, by mutual consent, no one speculated about the disappearance of Poppy Sullivan.

A few miles to the west Hoyt and Shirley were driving back to Tierra. For the first time in almost three years Hoyt thought about something besides the murder of Johnny Bradley. He had seen babies in the jungle, infants of peasants and partisans, but he hadn't learned enough Tagalog to share how they felt. He would go back to the Army in two weeks. He might go back to the Pacific. He might be sent to train special troops. He might be sent anywhere. He didn't know. He decided that he wouldn't think about it. For this day only, Hoyt let Johnny go, let the army go, and loved only the idea that he had been there when Will's baby was born.

Shirley, too, had let go. For the first time in many months the knitting needles of her mind did not scheme or fret over Will, over Virginia, or about her lot in life. It would be saying too much to say that she was taken with the birth of Virginia's child or that she had begun to consider the new possibility of who exactly would be in her future. It is enough to say that as Hoyt drove, Shirley slept. She was unaccustomed to being away from home and even more unaccustomed to being in a hospital or sitting with a soldier. But, as much as anything, she was unaccustomed to going all night without sleep. The regular thrum of the worn tires on the highway expansion joints lulled her to sleep, and eventually to seek a pillow, which took the form of Hoyt's right leg. The pickup rolled into Tierra in the early morning, both of them indifferent to whom might be watching from Nona's windows.

Shirley sat up and stretched her arms, then lay her head back down on Hoyt's lap. If Shirley had not been asleep she would have realized that it didn't look right.

Mrs. Tarlton did realize that it didn't look right. Her eyes darted around the café, at the ladies drinking coffee, the men telling stories, at the door which opened and closed, and at the highway. It was probably inevitable that she would see Hoyt Carter turn the family pickup off the road, cross Nona's parking lot, and angle toward the street that would lead to the center of town.

What's Hoyt doing coming from Clovis? Why do these boys want to spend all night over there at some road house?

Her questions were promptly answered by the sight of Shirley Fleming rising out of the seat next to Hoyt, stretching her arms to the ceiling of the pickup cab, yawning, smiling, undeniably disheveled.

Boys might go to Clovis to drink and chase around, but when a boy and a girl come driving back from Clovis at this hour of the morning, that only means one thing.

"My God," Mrs. Tarlton said in as plain and worldly a voice as she could muster for the crowd in the café. "Would you look at that!"

Everyone turned to look. Beyond Mrs. Tarlton, out the window, they saw what she saw. By nine-fifteen, before Shirley made it to her bedroom or Hoyt could drive out to the farm, every household in Tierra, Texas had been told that Shirley Fleming just eloped with Hoyt Carter.

"Good morning. How are we feeling today?"

Virginia hurt, to be sure, but she felt some unimagined sense of well-being and warmth that was completely independent of her sore body and torn bottom. She smiled up at the nurse, then reached her hands up to take her baby. The boy was a loud, thrashing bundle of blond sandy hair, red wrinkled skin, and closed eyes, screaming from the swaddling blanket the nurse had wrapped around him, as much for her protection as his.

"I believe this little tiger is hungry this morning. Are you ready to start?"

The nurse had helped Virginia loosen her gown and showed her the rudiments of preparing herself to be nursed, then helped her bring the little devil to her breast. It nuzzled at her, then attacked with a selfish frenzy that both hurt and made her laugh.

"Well, it looks like you're a natural little mother, like you were just made to have this baby." As she chatted the thing slurped and chomped with greedy abandon at Virginia's swollen bosom. "We need to fill out a birth certificate. I've got everything written down at one place or another. Six o'clock in the morning, assisted, weight five pounds six ounces, eighteen inches long, blond hair, blue eyes, mother, father. Foot prints, finger prints. Have you picked a name? No hurry, you've got plenty of time till we send you home but, when you're ready, we'll finish up the paper work.

"I've decided."

The thing continued to feed, noisily, through its mother's conversation.

"Oh, good. What are you going to call him?"

There had never been any doubt in Virginia's mind about what she would call this baby. The letters from France had only reinforced her decision. It was final.

"Peter. That's all. No middle name."

"Peter?"

"Yes, Peter. It would make his father proud. If he could be here."

The nurse smiled and made note of the name, then took a departing look at mother and child.

The smile had worn off by the time she got to the nurses' station. It had not been lost on her that this child was greedy. Greedy and loud.

Not the first time I've seen one like that, she reflected. She knew it was the kind of boy that would make life very hard on its mother.

The End

ABOUT THE AUTHOR

The **French Letters** series of novels are widely praised for their sense of America in the 1940s, both at home and in the Second World War. *Virginia's War* was a Finalist for Best Novel of the South and the Dear Author 'Novel with a Romantic Element' contest. *Engaged in War* won the silver medal at the London Book Festival for General Fiction and earned Author of The Year Honors for Jack Woodville London. The third novel in the series, *Children of a Good War,* is scheduled for publication.

Jack studied the craft of fiction at the Academy of Fiction, St. Céré, France and at Oxford University. He was the first Author of the Year of the Military Writers Society of America. He is the author of a number of published articles on the craft of writing and on early 20th Century history. His craft book, *A Novel Approach,* a short and light-hearted work on the conventions of writing, is designed to help writers who are setting out on the path to write their first book. *A Novel Approach* won the E-Lit Gold Medal for non-fiction in 2015.

Jack's work in progress is *Shades of the Deep Blue Sea,* a mystery-adventure novel about two sailors and a girl on a Pacific island that, instead of a tropical paradise, turns out to be a land of prisoner of war camps, cannibals who believe that God is singing to them from a military field radio, and an inconvenient Komodo dragon.

Jack lives in Austin, Texas. Visit him at jwlbooks.com or contact him at jack@jackwlondon.com.

www.ingramcontent.com/pod-product-compliance
Lightning Source LLC
Chambersburg PA
CBHW021012120726
47905CB00009B/2983